DAUGHTER
of the
REGIMENT

DAUGHTER
of the
REGIMENT

JACKIE FRENCH

Angus&Robertson
An imprint of HarperCollins*Publishers*

Angus&Robertson

An imprint of HarperCollins*Publishers*, Australia

First published in Australia in 1998
Reprinted in 1999
by HarperCollins*Publishers* Pty Limited
ACN 009 913 517
A member of the HarperCollins*Publishers* (Australia) Pty Limited Group
http://www.harpercollins.com.au

Text copyright © Jackie French 1998
Cover illustration copyright © Gwen Harrison 1998

Poem on page 84 'To Daffodils' written by Robert Harrick (1591–1674)

HarperCollins*Publishers*
25 Ryde Road, Pymble, Sydney, NSW 2073, Australia
31 View Road, Glenfield, Auckland 10, New Zealand
77-85 Fulham Palace Road, London W6 8JB, United Kingdom
Hazelton Lanes, 55 Avenue Road, Suite 2900, Toronto, Ontario M5R 3L2
and 1995 Markham Road, Scarborough, Ontario M1B 5M8, Canada
10 East 53rd Street, New York NY 10022, USA

National Library of Australia Cataloguing-in-Publication data:

French, Jackie.
Daughter of the regiment.
ISBN 0 207 19674 5
I. Title.
A823.3

Printed in Australia by Griffin Press Pty Ltd on 79gsm Bulky Paperback

10 9 8 7 6 5 4 3 2   99 00 01 02

For the people who love chooks. To Edward and Joseph, who breed Araucana chooks; to Kay Sagar, an unexpected chook lover; and to Catherine, Ian, Conor, Tarin, Marnie, Ashlee, Dani, Patricia, Rowan, Eleanor, Justin, Matthew, Jerome, Micah, Joel, Nick, Sam, Natalie, Sarah, Carleigh, Danni, Anne-Marree, Jack, Marg, John, Ashley, Amanda, David, Darcy and Mr J, who gave me the names of Harry's chooks . . . and to everyone else at Bolinda Primary School, with love.

Chapter 1

THE HOLE IN THE
CHOOK SHED

The chookhouse smelt of fresh droppings and laying mash and the slightly musty scent of feathers. The chookhouse always smelt, thought Harry. After it rained it smelt worse. When Dad had laid down fresh hay it smelt less; but it always smelt.

It wasn't a bad smell though, decided Harry, as he bent to collect the eggs. Sort of sweet, sort of . . . chooky.

The hens peered in the door behind him, hoping he'd brought down scraps. Chooks smelt sort of friendly, as long as the stink wasn't too strong.

'Shoo,' he said to a particularly persistent hen. That was Smokin' Joe, the old Isabrown. Smokin' Joe must be getting on for six years old, calculated Harry.

Dad had bought the Isabrown chickens the year the bushfires burnt Blaine's Gully. They'd thought Smokin' Joe was going to be a rooster. She'd even crowed a few times, the sort of strangled crow roosters make before they've learnt how to do it properly. But then she'd laid an egg.

Smokin' Joe pecked at Harry's feet, then looked up expectantly

'No, I haven't brought you anything you dopey chook,' declared Harry. 'I'm just collecting the eggs. Mum already brought the scrap bucket down this morning. Remember?'

Smokin' Joe paid no attention. She crouched on the dusty floor.

'Squark,' said Smokin' Joe.

'Do you want to jump up and lay an egg?' asked Harry. 'Is that what's wrong?' He stepped back from the laying boxes, the old ice-cream container full of eggs in his hand. 'Up you go then.'

It was silly to talk to chooks, but Harry reckoned everyone probably did it. Just not when there was anyone around to hear. 'I'm going to miss you if I have to leave next year Smokin' Joe. Will you miss me?'

Smokin Joe's tiny black eyes gazed at him. She

fluttered up into the old wooden fruit crate lined with hay that served as a laying box.

It'd be a brown egg, thought Harry. Isabrown chooks always laid brown eggs, brown as your knees in summer, just like Leghorns laid white ones and Australorps' eggs looked like they'd been dipped in milk with just a little chocolate added . . .

'Clurrrk,' said Smokin' Joe as she settled down.

In the next box old Sunset fluffed herself more firmly over her eggs. Sunset was an Araucana and laid blue eggs — tiny ones like they were made of painted china, not quite real. Everyone at school stared when Harry brought a blue hard-boiled egg for lunch.

Sunset's chickens would be half Araucana like Sunset, and half Australorp like Arnold Shwarzenfeather, the rooster. With a bit of luck Sunset's chickens might lay blue eggs like their mother, but really big ones, like Australorps. Sunset had been sitting for nearly two weeks now.

Smokin' Joe wriggled impatiently on the nest. Chooks didn't like anyone watching them lay.

'Lay a good big one, Smokin' Joe.' Harry turned to leave. 'Hey! What's that . . .?'

There was a light in the corner of the chookhouse, just below the perches. It pierced the gloom like a bit of sun had wandered in by mistake.

Harry stared at it. There must be a hole in the corrugated iron, he thought. A new hole with a sunbeam glancing through. Dad had made the chookhouse with the rusty old iron from the hay shed roof, so it was always getting holes.

Harry bent down under the perches. The light was incredibly bright in the dimness of the chookhouse. Surely the hole must be pretty large to let in so much light . . .

Harry looked up at the roof. If there was a really big hole up there the rain would splash in and the chooks might get wet. Of course, their feathers kept them warm, but they still didn't like to get wet.

The roof seemed okay. Harry looked at it more closely. No, there definitely wasn't a hole in the roof.

Harry ran his fingers over the walls. No holes there, either.

The light must be coming from somewhere. Not the door. It was at the wrong angle for the door. Harry peered at the light.

It wasn't really like a sunbeam at all. Sunbeams were long and slanting. This bit of light was round, like a hole on your jumper when the moths had been at it. It just sort of hung there, like it was a part of the dimness that someone had polished till it was bright. Almost as if it was solid.

He was being silly. Of course it wasn't solid . . .

Harry put his fingers up to touch it. See, he told himself. Your fingers pass right through.

Harry stopped. His fingers had disappeared.

Harry pulled his fingers back towards him. They

seemed alright, solid and slightly grubl
had just imagined . . .

Slowly, very slowly, Harry put his
towards the light. His fingers shone as they neared
it, went through it and . . .

And immediately they vanished.

Harry pulled his fingers back again, but slowly
this time, watching them reappear millimetre by
millimetre. He hadn't imagined it. When he put his
fingers into the light they vanished, and when they
came out of the light he could see them again.

Why?

Maybe the light was a whatsit ray, just like in that
movie . . . and everything it touched turned invisible.

Except his fingers weren't invisible. They were
still there. They only vanished when they were in the
light.

What was the light?

Harry looked at it closely. It was just light, that's
all. Just . . .

Except it wasn't. It wasn't just light. The closer
you got to it, the more you saw it was colour as well
as light. Lots of colours, like a rainbow squeezed
into the end of a plastic bag and all scrunched
together. A bit like a TV, thought Harry, shining in
the darkness from a distant room. Without thinking
Harry put his eyes up against the light.

What . . .! It was impossible. It couldn't be real . . .

The light wasn't light. Or rather it wasn't *just* light.

e light was a window, a tiny window onto . . .

What? thought Harry, as he peered into the hole. A window onto what?

There were trees through the hole, up on the hills above the creek flats. Not special trees, not magic trees. Not the sort of trees you'd see in another universe, perhaps. Just ordinary trees: manna gums and peppermints and a few red gums just like there were here, above the casuarinas along the creek.

The creek was like the one outside, except this other one had white-trunked gums along it instead of casuarinas, and there were waterlilies like splashes of white paint nudging at the boulders. It looked deeper, with soft, high grassy banks, and it was flowing more strongly. The water was clearer, too, so clear the clouds floated on the water like they were waterlilies.

Water like that would taste sweet, thought Harry. It'd feel like ice-cream on your skin when you swam in it.

The sky was blue, but a different colour blue to the blue outside the chookhouse. It was a deep midsummer blue, and high like a blown-up balloon so you'd think it would collapse if you pricked it. The sky today was cloudy, Harry remembered. A milky sort of blue.

There was nothing else. No animals. No people. No houses or aliens, or spaceships or cars. The trees rustled, a currawong called in the distance, but

Harry couldn't tell if the sounds came from the hole or from outside.

Harry took his eyes away. It was odd. Really odd. A sort of window in the chookhouse. But a window into what?

'Harry! Have you got the eggs?'

'Coming Mum,' yelled Harry.

He glanced one last time at the hole and galloped over the flat and up the path to the house. The old oaks squatted above him, as still in the heat as a chook on her nest. The giant agapanthus blooms stood like round blue soldiers of the guard along the path.

'Mum?'

'In here. I wish whoever finished the last of the toilet paper would get the next roll out. I remember your gran saying that if she had a penny for every roll of toilet paper she'd had to . . . just put the eggs on the table. I'll sort them out later.'

'Mum, there's something funny in the chook shed.'

His mother's face appeared around the bathroom door. 'Not that goanna again? If it takes one more egg I'm going to turn the hose on it.'

'No, it's a hole —'

His mother's face disappeared again. 'I'm not surprised. That tin leaked like a sieve when it was up on the shed roof. Tell your dad at dinner time.'

'No, Mum, not that sort of hole. It's a . . .'

'Oh blast it. There's the phone, and I wanted to get the accounts finished before dinner. It'll probably be your Aunt Gretchen wanting to tell me all about . . . what the . . . forget I said that word, Harry, you didn't hear it, now I've knocked the blessed fern out of its hanger. Get the phone will you, love? I'll be there as soon as I've put the poor thing back . . . oh look at all the mess . . .'

Chapter 2

Trying to Explain

'Dad?'

'Mmmm?' Dad looked up from his gravy. Dad was fond of gravy. He'd eat a pig and never notice its feet, Mum said, as long as it had gravy. 'Pass the potatoes will you, son? How was school? By the way, I meant to ask you, have you decided about boarding school yet?'

'No,' said Harry.

Dad's eyes sort of focused, as though his son was a farmer with 2,000 prime steers to sell, and he was wondering how to get the commission. Dad was the stock and station agent up in town. You always knew when Dad got that really friendly tone in his voice that he was trying to sell you something, thought Harry.

'I don't want to pressure you Harry,' Dad said earnestly. 'It's your choice whether you go or not. I've seen too many kids hate boarding school because they were forced to go. But just think of all the kids you'll meet up there — kids from all sorts of places —'

'Yeah,' muttered Harry.

'Not to mention all the subjects you can do,' said Mum. 'Chinese, Japanese, photography . . . you can't even take a language at all at Bradley's Bluff. Your cousin Elspeth is taking Indonesian now. It's her favourite subject, and her mother says . . .'

Wacko for Elspeth, thought Harry. He poked his silver beet over to the edge of his plate, and watched the thin green water trickle out onto the mashed potatoes.

Dad was silent for a moment. 'If you're not going to take up the place we really need to let the school know,' he said finally.

'I'm thinking about it,' said Harry shortly. 'Dad I saw something funny this afternoon. I mean really off. It's this hole in the chook shed.'

His father shrugged, and went back to his potatoes, carefully covering them with gravy before transferring them to his mouth. 'Well, there's not much I can do about it. I'm flat out at work at the moment. I've got three sales on next week and Stan'll be cutting the lucerne if the weather holds.' Dad and Grandad employed Stan Lennock to run their two farms. 'I haven't time to put a new roof on now and Stan certainly doesn't. A few holes won't hurt the chooks.'

'No, I mean a funny hole. A *really* funny hole.'

'That's what you said this afternoon,' remarked Mum. 'Harry, don't leave your silver beet on the side of your plate. Eat it. It's good for you. I don't know how you can expect to keep growing if you don't. What do you mean, a really funny hole?'

Harry took a breath. 'I don't quite know. I just thought it was an ordinary hole. Then I took a closer look at it, and I could see trees and the creek.'

Dad looked puzzled. 'But if you look through a hole in the chook shed that's what you do see — the trees and the creek.'

'But it wasn't *our* creek . . . it was like our creek, but different. And the trees were a bit different, too. I mean, there were the same sort of trees, but not the ones that are really there. And the hole wasn't in the wall of the shed. It was just hanging there.'

'A hole doesn't just hang there,' said Dad.

'This one does,' insisted Harry.

Mum frowned. 'Are you sure you're not making this up, Harry?'

'Course I'm sure. Come and look at it if you think I'm lying!'

'I don't think you're lying,' said Mum soothingly. 'Just maybe mistaken . . .' She glanced at Dad.

Dad put his fork down. 'Okay,' he said. 'Let's have a look at this hole.'

The garden smelt of freshly watered grass. The moon pushed its way effortlessly through the clouds, sending shadow dapples through the oak trees. It was hotter down on the flat below the garden. The grass shone dry and purple-gold in the moonlight.

Dad clicked off the torch. 'Don't need it,' he said. 'You could almost read a newspaper out here tonight.'

'Well, at least it'll make it easy to see this hole of yours,' said Mum. 'The moonlight will shine right through it.'

'Mum I tried to tell you — it isn't that sort of hole.'

Mum nodded.

The chook shed smelled stronger at night, Harry realised, the sort of smell that sawed down into your throat each time you breathed. The hens sat hunched and motionless, their dirty claws grasping the old bit of pipe Dad had nailed up as perches. They didn't even blink when the door opened.

'It's just over there,' said Harry. 'No, don't put the torch on, Dad. You'll see it better in the dark.'

'I don't see anything,' said Mum.

'It was here this afternoon!' Harry looked round the shed desperately. Maybe the hole had moved.

Dad clicked on the torch and shone it over the roof and walls. Spiders scuttled away, startled by the light. 'No new holes that I can see,' he said.

'But it WAS here,' insisted Harry. 'It was this funny golden light and it just hung there. I'm not lying. I'm not.'

'Of course you're not lying,' said Mum reassuringly. 'It was probably just one of the old holes that you hadn't noticed before.'

'But it just HUNG there —'

'Light can do funny things, son.' Dad clicked the torch off again. 'I remember an old shed — you know the one that used to be on Lagos's place before they built the new hay shed. I went in there one day and there was this great beam of light, like one of those laser things you see on TV and it was just coming through this pinhole in the ceiling.'

'But Dad. It wasn't *like* that. It wasn't coming from anywhere.'

'I remember when I saw a polar bear on the freeway just outside Sydney,' said Mum. She shut the door of the chookhouse behind her, and latched it. 'Do you remember that time, dear? Look, I yelled to your father, there's a polar bear in that Kombi van. But when he looked the van was gone, of course. I wondered for years about that polar bear, then one day I saw one again outside the supermarket in town ... but then when I went up close to it it was a dog, one of those Pyrennean Mountain dog things you see at the Show, and that must have been what I saw on the freeway, but I could have sworn it was a polar bear, just sitting up there beside the driver cool as you please ...'

It wasn't LIKE that, thought Harry stubbornly as he tramped across the flat behind them. It wasn't like that at all!

But there was no use trying to explain to Mum and Dad.

His room smelt of sweaty joggers and the summer jasmine twining up through the eaves outside the window. Harry couldn't sleep.

The hole HAD been there. He hadn't imagined it. He could still see the creek with its dappling of waterlilies, the sky that stretched forever, the thick-trunked trees. There were only a few as thick as that on the farm now. Most of them had been taken for fence posts or for timber last century.

Maybe the hole had moved. It hadn't seemed to move while he looked at it, but maybe it had shifted. After all, it hadn't been there yesterday afternoon. He'd been down at the shed for over an hour yesterday, just watching the chooks and wondering about boarding school — it always helped you think to look at chooks. He would have been sure to have seen it yesterday if it'd been there.

Maybe the hole moved really slowly. Maybe it was down by the creek now, or even over near the giant orange tree. If he crept out now he might find it . . .

Or maybe it really was a window to another world, and someone had shut the window. Though there hadn't been anyone inside the hole when he'd looked through it. . .

Or maybe . . .

A mopoke called — more pork, more pork — down by the swimming hole. It was funny, thought Harry drowsily, how you never heard mopoke's during the day. Maybe they thought their song would shrivel up in daylight. Or maybe sounds just travelled further at night.

Harry sat up. Night — of course! He'd been stupid. STUPID!

It had been daylight when he looked through the hole into the other world. Daylight here and daylight there. And now it was night here . . . so it could be night there as well . . . and there'd be no golden light glowing through the hole at night. There'd be only darkness, imperceptible in the darkness here.

Harry lay down again. Tomorrow first thing he'd go down to the chookhouse. No, not first thing — there wasn't time before the bus to school. Straight after school then, when he had time to really look at the hole. It had to be there then, it had to!

Chapter 3

CISSIE

The school bus snaked down the road to the valley. Harry called it the Spaghetti Road — from up on the tableland it looked just like a piece of spaghetti that someone had dropped on the floor.

'Three whole days off school,' Spike stretched in satisfaction. 'Whoever invented pupil-free days should be given a medal. Coming swimming this afternoon?'

Harry shook his head. 'I've got some jobs at home,' he answered evasively.

'Too bad.' Spike stretched his toes out into the

aisle. 'Dad says it's building up to a thunderstorm. The water might be too cold to swim tomorrow.'

'It's always cold.'

'It gets colder after it's rained though.'

'Yeah. Pity,' agreed Harry. He gazed out the window impatiently. Shorn paddocks of brown stubble, with scattered bales of hay still greenish-gold. Paddocks of tough, thin cocky's bootstraps with the sheep looking enviously at the lusher grass next door; Dwyer's place and Steinler's . . .

The bus seemed to take forever. *Everyone* was on the bus today. The bus stopped at almost every letterbox. There was a box of lemons to drop off to Mrs Albertstein at Woolly Corner, and everyone had to peer out the windows at Melissa Forrest's joey which her mum had brought down to the bus stop in its hessian sack. Couldn't Mac drive faster?

'Got much homework?'

Harry shook his head. Surely the bus usually went faster than this?

'Sure you can't come for just a quick swim?' asked Spike again, as the bus pulled in to his and Angie's stop. The swimming hole down at their place was bigger than the one up at Harry's, though Harry's had a smooth rock you could slide down and splash into the water.

Harry shook his head. 'No. Thanks anyway.'

'It's not as much fun just swimming with Angie,' Spike complained as he hauled himself out of his seat. 'See you Tuesday. Hey, how about a swim Sunday then? Or Monday? We've got to go to Aunt Mag's Saturday, it's Uncle Finn's birthday or something, but we could come up to your place Sunday if you like.'

'Yeah, sure,' agreed Harry. Anything to get him moving off the bus. 'See you Sunday. See you Sunday, Angie.'

'What's on Sunday?' demanded Angie, dragging her bag up the passageway from the back where she'd been making faces out the back window with the other girls.

'We're going up to Harry's place for a swim in the afternoon . . .'

Harry watched them straggle off the bus. Mac turned the wheel again and pulled out into the dusty road. Only one more stop now . . .

The chooks looked at him with interest as he walked up the flat, hoping for wheat. Humans meant food. The scrap bucket in the morning: leftover porridge or baked potatoes or yesterday's stale sandwiches. Or wheat or corn at night, a final treat before they were locked inside to keep them safe from foxes.

Arnold Shwarzenfeather gave a half blast crow — the sort that meant, Food alert! Food alert! Possible food coming! Get it together girls! (A full-throated crow meant, Warning! Warning! Pay attention now!)

'Buzz off,' said Harry. He stepped over Midnight

Sky and Omelette and Mr J (they always crowded at your ankles so they wouldn't miss a thing) and peered into the chookhouse.

No chooks in the boxes, except for Sunset, broody in the corner. Chooks mostly laid their eggs in the morning, except for Smokin' Joe . . . yes, there was her egg, dark brown against the hay. Smokin' Joe must have been in already this afternoon. Harry stepped through the door and peered between the perches.

The hole was in the corner, just where it had been the day before.

Harry stared at it. Of course he'd known it would be there, he'd been sure it would be there — but it was still amazing that it really *was* there. It glowed as strongly as before.

Harry glanced behind him. No sign of Mum or Dad. Should he yell for them to come down and see it, in case it disappeared again? Or should he have a closer look at it first? Just to make sure it really was as weird as it had been the day before, that the other world really was inside it.

Harry bent under the perches. He craned his head up and put his eyes to the hole.

The other world was still there. It looked just the same, except today the sky was cloudy — pale grey cloud stretched tight as speedos across the sky. The creek shone grey as well. He could almost hear it whisper between the rocks . . . was it the creek through the hole or his creek outside? He could hear trees brush their leaves against the wind.

Hey, what was that? It sounded like laughter. Was it coming from the hole? Maybe someone was laughing up at the house, or in the garden. Or was it Stan laughing up in the big shed?

Harry crawled back under the perches and stuck his head outside. The chooks clucked curiously; a currawong yelled in the tree above. The house, the sheds, the grassy flat, the garden were quiet.

Harry crawled back inside. The laughter was definitely coming from the hole. It was louder now, as though whatever made the sound was coming closer, closer, closer . . .

Harry put his eye back to the hole.

The creek still rippled in the other world. The clouds still stretched featureless across the sky. Harry blinked.

There was a girl among the trees on the other side of the creek. She wore a long skirt and her blouse was long-sleeved although the day looked warm, and a funny-looking hat so it was hard to see her face. The girl laughed again, and spun around, around and around and around . . .

'Hello? Hello? Can you hear me?' Harry felt stupid calling through a hole . . . but if he could hear her, maybe she could hear him?

The girl's skirts swirled faster.

'Can you hear me?' Harry yelled louder.

Suddenly the girl collapsed in a giggling heap among the trees.

'Cissie!' It was a man's voice. It sounded like he was laughing as well, though Harry couldn't see him. 'I *said* you'd make yourself giddy if you whirled like that!'

The girl lay back on the grass. She was much younger than he was, Harry realised, about five perhaps, or six. Her hair hung in two plaits down both shoulders. It was blonde hair, tied with blue ribbons at the ends. 'The sky is going round and round and round!' she called.

'That's because you were going round and round.' It was a woman's voice now, warm and amused. 'Come on, sillyhead. If you don't come now we'll have eaten all the cake.'

The girl sat up. What had the man called her? wondered Harry. Cissie, that was it.

'Cake! Is there cake?' she cried. 'What sort of cake, Mama?'

'Currant cake.' It was the man's voice now. 'Your mama used the last of the currants too, and there won't be any more till the supply ship comes, and who knows when that will be.'

The girl — Cissie — leapt to her feet. Her first step was unsteady. She blinked then oriented herself. She ran in the direction of the voices.

Blast! Harry tried to crane his head around to see her. But no matter which way he turned he could only see straight ahead in the hole and not to either side.

'Can I have that piece?'

'Greedy reedy. You'll have the piece you're given, miss.'

'Yes Papa.' But the voice was hopeful, not repentant.

The woman laughed. 'Give her the big slice, John.'

Cissie laughed again, and suddenly she was back in view, leaping up onto the largest rock, hardly hampered by her skirts. She sat down on the rock's flat top, arranging her skirts around her, and began to eat. Her shoes were funny, thought Harry. Sort of boots and all buttoned up to the ankle.

'Papa?'

'Yes, Cissie?'

'Why is the sky blue?'

Harry almost laughed. It was just the sort of question a little kid like that might ask.

'I don't know, my dear. Maybe you should ask Captain Piper. He knows the answer to everything.'

The woman laughed. 'John! Don't you encourage her to ask the Captain a question like that. She probably will now!'

'He won't mind,' said the man's voice.

'She's being thoroughly spoilt, that's what she is.' But the woman's voice was indulgent. 'The only child here. Everyone treats her like a pet kitten. Sergeant Wilkes carving her that doll and the o'possum skin Lieutenant Burrows brought back for her and . . .'

'And the feathers he brought back for you, for your hat. You're the queen of the garrison, Mrs Harrington, my love, you and Mrs Sorrell, but she can't hold a candle to you. I should be jealous . . .' There was more laughter suddenly and words he couldn't catch.

'Papa! Look!'

'Look at what, my pet?'

'That tree! Look, there's a face on it!'

Harry looked. The kid was right. There was a face, shaped by the gnarled bark on the trunk of the tree.

'It looks a kind face,' decided Cissie. 'I like this place. It's the best place in the whole world. Who owns it, Papa? The black people?'

'His Majesty the King owns it now, pet.'

'Why? Did he buy it from them?'

Her mother laughed. 'The questions you ask, Cissie! Who ever heard of a question like that!'

'But King William owns EVERYTHING! I mean who REALLY owns it?'

'No one then. Not yet.'

'Can it be mine, Papa?

'Of course,' assured the man.

'John!' The woman's voice was laughing again. 'She really will think it's hers!'

'I think this place should be mine, because I love it best,' decided Cissie. 'Much more than King

William. Besides, King William likes the sea, doesn't he, Papa? Captain Piper said he was the sailor king. He'd think this pool was much too small. Papa, can I bathe?'

'It's too cold. Besides, it's past time we were getting back.'

'But Papa!'

'Don't argue, Cecilia,' said the man.

Cissie wrinkled her nose and brushed the crumbs from her skirt. Would the man and woman come into view now? wondered Harry. But they didn't. Cissie jumped to her feet and began to leap from rock to rock along the creek. Her boots clicked and slid on the granite. The voices grew more distant and the laughter; then the laughter merged with bird calls.

Then it was gone.

Harry stayed with his eye to the hole. But they didn't return.

It was hot in the chookhouse, the smells more pungent in the heat. Harry's neck was cramped. His knees hurt from kneeling above the muck.

'Harry! Harry, where are you?'

'Here! I'm here, Mum!' Harry straightened his knees painfully and clambered out of the chookhouse.

Mum came down the garden steps onto the flat. 'I saw your bag but didn't know where you were.'

'I was in the chookhouse.'

'Looking for your hole?' Mum smiled.

'Yes. It's . . .' Harry halted. All he had to do was take Mum over to it, and she'd see it for herself. But something stopped him.

Maybe it was the laughter. It had been such private laughter, the girl and her parents believing they were alone. He'd eavesdropped and he wasn't sure he wanted anyone else to eavesdrop as well. Besides, it was his world, that funny world inside the light.

And suddenly he realised he didn't want anyone else to share it. Not even Mum and Dad.

'Yeah,' he said finally. 'You were right, Mum. It was just a trick of the light. There's this little hole on the wall and the light shines right through it.'

'I told you it'd be something like that,' said Mum sympathetically. 'Come on. It's hot enough to melt a mountain out here. You'll be getting heatstroke, just like Uncle Ron did that time down at the coast when we were kids . . . did I ever tell you about that? Come and have some afternoon tea.'

Chapter 4

TRYING TO MAKE
SENSE OF IT

He dreamed of the girl that night. Cissie, that was her name. Cissie.

In his dream she was laughing, among the rocks, the creek muttering beyond her, the ripples wrinkling the red gum shadows on the water. Then suddenly the laughter stopped. There was silence, the sort that seemed to echo even though there was no noise, and then the sound of sobbing, sobbing, sobbing . . .

Harry woke up shivering. His doona had slipped sideways in the night. He was cold, that was all. He'd had a nightmare because he was cold.

Harry pulled the doona up over his shoulders again and twitched the curtain aside. The sky was grey, not black. A cuckoo trilled down the scale like it was practising for an eisteddfod. Arnold Shwarzenfeather would be crowing soon, and then the kookaburras would be gurgling, and the shrike thrush singing and then every other bird around would yell up at the sky.

There was no way he could get back to sleep. The dream was still too strong.

That small girl by the creek, crying, crying, crying, all alone.

But that was silly. Silly. She'd been laughing. Her parents had been with her. She'd been having fun, not unhappy at all. They'd all been picnicking by the creek which was so like his creek . . .

Harry sat up, the doona slipping from his shoulders. Of course!

It WAS his creek! Cissie's creek was his creek like it must have been last century perhaps, before the gold miners dredged it and sieved it searching for their gold . . . the gold miners came in 1852 so it had to be before that. Maybe twenty years before or even more.

Mrs Easton at school said there'd been waterlilies all along the creek in those days, and giant red gums along the banks, instead of just a few skinny ones on the creek flats. The miners had cut down the red gums to fuel their dredges and the casuarinas had taken their place.

Hadn't Mrs Easton said there'd been a garrison here in the early days, even before the farmers came? The soldiers had been stationed down by the river in case the French invaded, in case they sailed up from the sea with their cannons and their flag to claim the land, just as the English had claimed it a few years before . . . but no French ship ever came.

Cissie's father must have been one of the soldiers at the garrison, and her mother and Cissie lived there as well. And that Captain Piper they spoke about, and Sergeant Wilkes . . . and there would have been more soldiers stationed at the garrison if they were there to keep out the French.

It would have been a lonely outpost in those days. It took weeks of trekking on horseback from Sydney to get there in the days before roads and cars and planes, unless you had a boat, and how many boats were there back then?

So, thought Harry, that's what he was seeing through the hole. This place more than a hundred and fifty years ago. What was the hole then? A hole in time? Could Cissie see him . . . was there a hole at her end as well? There had to be . . . but she hadn't seemed to see it. Maybe she was too upset to see the hole.

Or maybe. . . yes, Harry realised, that was it. He'd seen the hole because it was bright in the dimness of the chookhouse — but on Cissie's side it'd just be another patch of daylight with daylight all around. You'd have to be right up against it to see that it was different. You didn't hear anything from the hole unless you were right up close as well.

Maybe there were lots of holes like that, thought Harry drowsily, as though time rubbed thin just *there* and you never noticed. You just walked on straight past . . .

He must have slept. The next thing he knew Arnold Schwarzenfeather was yelling from the chookyard and Dad was singing in the shower.

Breakfast was always late on Saturdays. Dad had to go into work till lunchtime, and Mum usually went with him, but they didn't open till eight-thirty or even nine, so there was no point eating early.

Dad fried bacon and eggs. He always cooked Saturday breakfast — Australorp eggs for him because he liked them best, and Isabrowns for Harry, and a white Leghorn egg for Mum.

Harry squeezed the oranges that came from the giant tree on the flat. The juice was yellow. It looked more like lemon cordial than the orange juice in bottles.

The tree had been planted over a hundred years ago, when orange trees grew into huge things, almost as tall as gums, not like the small neat modern trees at all. The oranges were hard and tiny, and always freckled (sometimes if you rubbed them off onto your skin the freckles stayed there till you washed them away), but the juice tasted better than the stuff from the supermarket. Or maybe you just liked what you were used to, thought Harry. He'd always drunk the juice from the fruit of the trees on the flat.

'What do you plan for today?' asked Dad. His hand hovered between the honey and the plum jam. 'Coming into town with us? We could pick up a video if you like.' He unscrewed the lid of the plum jam and began to spread it thickly on his toast.

Harry shook his head. 'I've got a lot of homework,' he said. 'I'll just get it over with this morning if that's okay.'

'Sure,' said Dad, surprised. Harry usually left his homework till just before bedtime on Sundays, then panicked because he couldn't get it all done. 'Do you want us to pick up a video for you?'

'Oh thanks,' said Harry. 'Any one . . . Hey Mum, can I take the scrap bucket down to the chooks.'

Mum blinked. 'Thank you,' she said.

'No worries,' said Harry. 'I'll take it down every morning if you like. It can be one of my jobs, like collecting the eggs.'

Mum smiled. 'I'll still have it to do it myself next year, if you're off to school.'

Harry shrugged.

Chapter 5

THE HOLE IN TIME

The chooks strutted and clucked inside the netting, impatient to get out for the day's pecking around the flat, scratching under the blackberries for beetles and fallen caterpillars, wriggling ecstatically into the dust under the lavender bushes. It must be hard to be a chook where they made you stay inside all day, thought Harry.

He unlatched the wire gate and propped it open. If you didn't prop the gate open it might swing shut and then the chooks couldn't get back in at night, and flew up to the trees instead. Once chooks got used to roosting somewhere it was hard to get them to change their minds. Chooks weren't very bright, Harry guessed. The chooks clustered round him, unwilling to leave till they'd feasted on the contents of the scrap bucket.

Harry tipped it out at the far end of the run — two banana peels, half a piece of toast and plum jam, congealed gravy, a mouldy end of cheese, a quarter of a loaf of stale bread, his lunchtime apple that Kevin Briggs had trodden on yesterday, potato peelings, silver beet stalks and outer lettuce leaves, pumpkin peel and seeds, six bacon rinds, half a piece of fruit cake (where had that come from, wondered Harry — he hadn't known they had a fruit cake), tea leaves and three crushed eggshells (Mum crushed them so the chooks wouldn't get the idea of eating the eggs).

The chooks began to scratch the pile apart, pecking first at the cheese and bread and leaving the greenery till later.

Harry checked their water (still flowing well) and their food container (still half full), then hesitated. He was almost scared to look through the hole this morning. But of course there was nothing to be scared of. Cissie had been happy yesterday. The sadness was just a dream.

The chooks were still busy with the scraps at the end of the run. Harry peered through the gloom of the chookhouse. Faintly, in the distance, he could hear the sound of the ute bumping across the ramp as Mum and Dad headed off to town.

The hole was still there. He'd half hoped it wouldn't be, but it was shining just the same behind the perches.

Harry ducked, making sure he didn't bump his head on the perches. Someone would be sure to notice if his hair was mucky and ask why. Harry pressed his eye to the hole.

There was no one there.

What had he expected? Harry thought, almost in relief. Of course there was no one there. They'd only been there yesterday for their picnic. They'd all be back at the garrison today. He'd probably never see Cissie again; never see anything again through the hole, except the creek and trees.

Wait a second — something moved on the far side of the creek. It leapt out of a bush, then bounded down along the creek bank, out of sight.

Harry grinned. A wallaby. Maybe it was the zillion times great-grandaddy of the wallaby who lived nowadays over on the flat on the other side of the creek. He could see a wallaby any day he wanted to, without glueing his eye to a hole . . .

Someone was coming! That's why the wallaby had fled. Perhaps it was Cissie and her parents again. Perhaps it was someone else from the camp.

It was Cissie. But she looked different, thought Harry. She was taller, surely, than she'd been yesterday. How could she have grown so much taller in just a day?

Maybe it hadn't been just a day for her, Harry realised. She looked at least eight now, or nine. Maybe more time had passed in her world.

Cissie came closer. She'd been crying. Her face was swollen, her eyes were red. She breathed in funny shaking gulps, as if it was hard to run and cry as well. She sank onto the rock where she had sat the day before — or had it been two years before, or more — and sobbed.

It was like his dream, and yet it wasn't. The dream had been indistinct, as though reality wobbled to and fro. But this was real.

What was wrong? wondered Harry. Had someone hurt her? Had she quarrelled with her parents? What had happened? Harry pressed his mouth close to the hole.

'Hello!'

There was no response from the other side of the hole. He tried again. 'Hello! Cissie! Cissie, can you hear me?'

The girl kept sobbing.

It was no use. It was just like it had been yesterday. He could hear her, but she couldn't hear him. But there must be something he could do to help. Her sobs sounded so desolate.

'Cissie? Cecilia, love.' The voice sounded out of breath.

'Papa?' The girl looked up. Both she and Harry had been too intent to hear him come. 'Papa . . . I . . . I'm sorry I ran. I just couldn't stay there. I just kept on running . . .'

'It's all right, Cissie love. I understand.' The man stepped into view.

Cissie's father was short, thought Harry. Why had he thought a soldier must be tall? He had black hair that stuck up like he had run his hands through it, and bushy side whiskers that nearly met at his chin. He looked like he had been crying, too. Did soldiers cry? He knelt by the girl and took her into his arms. 'Mama is with the angels now.'

Harry froze under the perches. 'No,' he thought. 'Oh no . . .'

'I don't want the angels to have her!' cried Cissie. 'She's mine, not their's! I want her here. She shouldn't have gone away.'

'But she can't be here, my love. She would be if she could.'

Cissie nodded without speaking. The man stroked her hair. 'We must go back. They were worried about you. Sergeant Wilkes has made a johnnycake for your supper.'

'I couldn't eat, Papa.'

'He wants to be kind,' said the man. 'Try to eat it for him, Cissie. It's all he knows what to do to help.'

Cissie nodded. She took his hand. They walked together down the creek.

The sun glared down outside the chook shed. Harry sat by the creek where Cissie had sat, so many years ago. He wished Mum and Dad would come back, but somehow he wanted to be alone as well.

That poor little girl, crying on the rock. It must be terrible to have your mother die — especially in a strange place.

What must it be like to lose your mother in a strange land, wondered Harry. Because Australia *must* be strange to Cissie. She'd have come here from England, or maybe Scotland or Ireland . . . no, it would be England. Her accent hadn't been Scots or Irish. Harry calculated . . . no, he was wrong, she might have been born here. Maybe this place hadn't been so strange to her at all . . . but still, how horrible . . . how hard for a kid to bear . . .

If only he could help her. But he couldn't. She looked so close, but she was far away. A hundred and fifty years away. All he could do was watch.

He should go back. He should watch again. Next time it wouldn't be so bad. Maybe she wouldn't be so unhappy next time. You'd never get over your mother's death . . . but happy things would happen too. Maybe she'd be laughing again, next time. Her father might marry again, someone really nice and . . .

He had to go back. He had to see what happened next.

Chapter 6

WHAT HAPPENS NEXT?

Harry went back into the chookhouse. A tomato seedling was already growing out of the pile of chook manure just outside the door that he'd scraped out last weekend. (Mum said his nan had told her that chook manure was the best thing ever for the roses.) The nesting boxes were full. Midnight Sky, the Australorp, and Hazelnut, the Rhode Island Red, and Smokin' Joe all glared at him with tiny shining eyes.

'Sorry,' said Harry.

Squarrkk! yelled Smokin' Joe. She flung herself

out of the nest and ran shrieking down the flat. Arnold Shwarzenfeather trotted a few steps after her then, realising she was all right, strutted back into the shade of the oak trees.

'Dumb chook,' said Harry. He glanced down at the egg in the nest, dark brown and still warm from Smokin' Joe's body. She laid good eggs though, thought Harry.

The hole shone in the corner. It didn't look quite so noticeable at the moment. The rest of the chookhouse was too light. It was only in the afternoon when the chookhouse grew dimmer that the light seemed to shine so brightly. Harry stepped over to it reluctantly. He squatted on the dusty floor, and pressed his eyes to the hole.

She was there. She was a little older perhaps, her hair perhaps a little darker, like hay a week after it's been cut. She sat on her rock, just as she had before.

She was reading a book, but the scene was too far away for Harry to be able to read the title. She pulled at one of the plaits and nibbled the end of it — just like that little kid in Year Three who bit the end of her plaits sometimes, thought Harry.

The creek swirled around her, sending the waterlilies wobbling in the current. It must have rained a little while before, thought Harry; not enough for a flood but a freshening. The water still looked clear. In Harry's day the water turned muddy after even a little rain, the topsoil from the paddocks upstream washing down it.

'Say something,' muttered Harry. 'How do I know if you're happy or not? Say something!'

The girl was silent, reading her book.

She must come here often, thought Harry. It was her spot, her special place. She'd come here when she was unhappy, and she came here just to read or think as well.

Harry scratched the back of his neck absently. One of the chooks must have mites . . . something had to happen soon! He could feel it!

Cissie laid down her book and yawned. She stretched.

She didn't look unhappy, thought Harry. She didn't look particularly happy either. She just looked bored. Perhaps it was a dull book. Did she have to do lessons, he wondered? How had she learnt to read if she didn't go to school?

Cissie bent and picked up the book. She stuck her tongue out at it. Yes, thought Harry, it probably was a lesson book. She lifted her skirts with both hands, longer skirts now — they came almost to her ankles. Before Harry realised what had happened she had leapt from her rock with her book and was gone.

Harry leant back from the hole. He had been so sure something momentous was going to happen! But at least she was okay. At least she wasn't crying. After all, everyone was bored some of the time.

Maybe the next time she'd be happy.

Everyone got their own lunch on Saturdays. Harry spread chunks of bread with tomato and cheese and black olives — sort of like a cold pizza, except he never could get the bread to cut straight. Mum and Dad listened to the weather report on the radio. Harry sat down quietly at the kitchen table so as not to interrupt.

'Looks like that low over the Bight will miss us,' said Dad, and took his plate to the sink. 'Pity — we could do with the rain. I wouldn't be surprised if we get a thunderstorm though. It's building up to it. Is there any more cheese left, love?'

'In the fridge,' said Mum. 'I bought some of that stuff we had at Sally's, you know, you said you liked it . . . Did you get your homework done, Harry?'

'Not all of it,' said Harry, guiltily. 'I'll finish it later.'

'I picked up a video,' said Dad. 'It looks pretty good. I might watch it with you tonight.'

'Sure,' said Harry. 'That'd be cool. Dad, I was wondering. Would you mind if I made another chook run?'

'If you like.' Dad sounded surprised. 'Where do you want to put it?'

'On the end of the old one, I think. Just to give them more space. I'm not sure. I might just poke around down there and get some ideas.' It would give him an excuse for being down at the chookhouse all the time.

'There's some old wire in the shed if you need it,' said Dad. 'Sing out if you want a hand.'

'I'll be right,' said Harry. He prodded at his sandwich. How could he eat when who knows what might be happening down at the chookhouse? 'Hey, can I be excused?'

'But you've hardly eaten anything!' protested Mum. 'Do you feel all right Harry? Come over here and let me feel your forehead. Maybe you had too much sun. Linda at the checkout said this morning there was a wog going round. Two of her kids have had it and —'

'Mum . . . Mum, I'm fine.' Harry broke away 'Really. Just not hungry.'

Chapter 7

CAPTAIN PIPER

It was going to rain tonight for sure, realised Harry, as he stepped outside onto the verandah. The air sort of pricked at your skin, and was almost too dense to breathe. The sky was a high pale blue, as if it had been washed a lot. Was that why he'd felt that something was going to happen earlier? It was just the coming storm.

Down on the flat the hens raced in widening circles, pecking newly-hatched flying termite queens out of the air. Soon the termites would lose their wings, thought Harry, and scurry down into shelter.

He watched as Midnight Sky flapped her wings, half flying up to grab a high one.

The termites only flew when it was going to rain. Sometimes it might be just a sprinkle, half damp, half dust; other times a downpour; but the termites always knew.

The ants would probably be frantic, too, scurrying in and out of their holes, erecting sandy barriers against a flood, and yes — there were a pair of golden skinks, tearing at each others' throats. Lizards always got niggly before a storm. That meant a thunderstorm, then, not just a gentle rain . . .

It was hard to breathe in the chookhouse, as though the coming storm had sucked out all the air. Even the world through the hole looked breathless, as though a storm was building there as well. The water rippled and nibbled at the edges of the rocks, as if they would like to bite them but weren't sure how.

Cissie was there. Somehow Harry had known that she'd be there. She gazed at the creek, though it was the sort of look, thought Harry, that didn't really see what was in front of you. She chewed her plait again. And then her face screwed up and she began to sob, resting her head against her arms upon the rock.

It was the most desolate sound that Harry had ever heard.

No! It wasn't fair! Things couldn't be bad for her

now. Not again! Things had to be getting better! Cissie deserved to be happy now!

The sobs echoed from the rocks, the trees. They seemed to clutch at him, tear at him; he was no longer in his world, but in hers. What was wrong! It had to be something big, something important. You didn't cry like that for a torn dress, or if you'd got your homework wrong.

If only he *could* cross over to Cissie's world, just for a while, just long enough to comfort her . . . or to bring her here, to Mum.

'Cissie! Cecilia! Where are you, child?'

The girl's head rose. 'Captain Piper? I'm over here.' Her voice was hoarse with tears.

There was a man in the distance, but the hole was so small it was hard to make him out. He came closer, striding confidently through the shadows, and now Harry could see him clearly.

He was taller than Cissie's father. He wore a uniform of some kind, or part of a uniform anyway. A faded red coat with some sort of braid at the shoulders and a white shirt open at the neck. His boots were long and black and shiny, but even from Harry's vantage point you could see they were worn right down at the heel, and one was patched up towards the top.

'Cissie, my dear, we've been looking everywhere for you. You shouldn't have run away like that.' The man's voice was kind.

'I know.' It was a whisper. 'I'm sorry, Captain Piper.'

'They've taken your papa to the mortuary, child,' said Captain Piper. 'He's at peace now, Cissie. He's in heaven with your mama.'

No!

The man's words screamed in Harry's mind. Not her father! Not her father, too! The shock was so great he hardly heard Cissie's next words.

'I know.' The girl's voice was very low.

'It's all right, child,' said Captain Piper gently. 'We'll look after you. Your father had good friends in the regiment. We'll keep you safe.'

'Thank you. Thank you, Captain Piper.' Harry could hardly hear her voice.

'Come on now. Mrs Sorrel has some bread and milk for you.'

'I . . . I wouldn't want to bother Mrs Sorrel. Not when she's had the fever, too.'

'It's no bother.' Captain Piper smiled slightly. 'You two are the only women here now. She needs you too, Cissie.'

The girl nodded. She smoothed her plaits. She took the Captain's hand and they walked back through the trees.

Harry sat in silence in the chook shed. It was some time before he felt able to come out.

That night the dream came again.

Harry burrowed his head into the pillow, trying

to convince himself the crying was the gurgle of the rain pouring into the water tank, an owl yelling above the storm . . .

But it was Cissie.

He had to find her, but the hole was gone! He hunted through the chookhouse, but still it wasn't there!

He had to find it! He had to! He had to comfort Cissie . . . then suddenly the hole was back and he was peering through but still he couldn't see her. The world was grey and blurred as though the colours had melted all together.

Someone had to help her! It couldn't be him. He was too far away. No matter how he tried he couldn't touch her, speak to her, or comfort her! If only Captain Piper, Sergeant Wilkes . . .

But this time no one came to find her. Cissie kept crying, crying, crying through the years . . .

Chapter 8

SUNDAY

Harry had to force himself to go down to the chook shed on Sunday morning, but the bucket of scraps was ready for the chooks. Part of him longed to go, the other was afraid of what he might see. Surely the worst had happened to her now, surely things must get better now!

But what would she do, orphaned, so alone? What was this Mrs Sorrel like? Was she good to her? Was her husband a soldier at the garrison as well? He must be. There was no one except the soldiers there . . . and Cissie.

Maybe the Sorrels would adopt her. Maybe Captain Piper had a wife and she'd come to look after Cissie . . . maybe, maybe, maybe . . .

If only it was a story or a movie. If only you could say: It should have happened like *that*, and make it true. But this was real! This was all happening . . . no, it had *already* happened, all those years ago.

You couldn't change it now. You couldn't say: That isn't right! and bring her parents back, and see her laugh again . . .

The creek lapped and gurgled after the rain, so fresh you could hear it right up on the steps. Even the grass looked greener, as though it had changed colour as soon as it smelt the damp. The flying termites were gone.

The laying boxes were full of chooks. Sunset still fluffed down firmly on her eggs, but the other boxes were full as well; Midnight Sky in one and Sky Maze in another, and both Moonlight and Chickenpox trying to cram into the third.

There was enough room — just, thought Harry — if they both kept their wings to themselves. He'd even seen three chooks in one nest last year. The third one sort of perched right up over the others, so the egg would fall between.

It must feel funny to know you had to lay an egg nearly every other day. Did they think about it much, or did they suddenly remember, Hey, I need to lay?

He was putting off looking through the hole. But he had to look. No matter how bad it was, he had to see what happened next. The chooks glared at him reproachfully from their laying boxes.

The pool through the hole was still, the waterlily leaves flat and placid along the edges. There were no waterlily flowers today. A snake weaved like a streak of oil through the rocks, then slipped into the water without a ripple. It swam with its head out of the water for a moment, then ducked deep into the coolness below.

Voices! There were voices in the distance!

For a moment he thought it might be Cissie coming back. But they were men's voices, laughing at a joke he couldn't hear. How could they laugh when Cissie was so unhappy?

Was she still unhappy? How much time had passed?

Suddenly Harry saw them, pale among the shadows, two men in buff-coloured trousers, and shirts that were lighter still. Closer, closer, till they were almost directly in front of him.

'Here's as good a place as any,' said one of them. 'It's a likely enough pool, I'll warrant.' He was Dad's age perhaps, with tanned skin like Dad's and long shaggy sideburns and dark blue eyes.

The other man nodded. He was Grandad's age or even older, Harry reckoned. His sideburns were mostly reddish–grey. He carried a bundle which looked like a blanket. He unrolled it without speaking and Harry saw it was a net, with a rope along the top and weighted down with stones on the bottom.

'You take that end,' instructed the first man.

They handled the net like they were used to it, thought Harry, dropping it in at the head of the swimming hole, right where Harry kept his lilo one hundred and fifty years later. Each man held an end as they dragged it along the swimming hole, dislodging the waterlilies so they bunched unevenly across the net.

Harry realised they were fishing. There were probably lots of fish in the swimming hole in their day, though you hardly ever saw a fish nowadays. The creek had never really recovered from the gold mining.

Something jumped in front of the net, brown and silver in the sunlight, then splashed back into the water. The first man laughed. 'That's the way of it,' he called. 'We've got them now!'

The older man knelt down and pulled at the bottom of the net and suddenly the whole thing was out of the water.

The fish were BIG, Harry saw. He'd no idea there'd ever been fish that big in the creek . . . six or eight of them at least, wriggling and squirming till at last they grew still.

'A good enough catch,' said the first man. The

second nodded. He didn't seem to talk much, thought Harry. He grabbed one end of the net as his companion took up the other, so they carried it like a giant fish-filled sling between them.

'Think she'll like this little lot?' asked the first man.

The second man shrugged, then spoke for the first time. His voice was hoarse, like he yelled too often and had worn it away. 'I don't reckon she'll like anything much today,' he said. 'Not with her Pa so new in his grave.'

They were talking about Cissie, Harry realised. They were hoping Cissie might like a fish.

'Still and all, it's a change from kangaroo,' said the first. 'What I wouldn't give for a cut off the joint now. A giant beef sirloin all dripping juice, and a pudding with the gravy, and all the trimmings. Makes your mouth water doesn't it, Wilkes?'

Wilkes grunted.

'Not that there's a chance of a sirloin here, not in this forsaken place. The sooner the recall comes, the better for me. It's all right for you, Wilkes, with nobody waiting for you. I've got my Becky at home and it's been six years since I've seen her.'

'She could've come out here,' said Wilkes in his rough voice.

'I'd like to see my Becky in a place like this. Look what it's done to Mrs Sorrel, to that poor kid's mama! It's no place for a woman out here.'

Wilkes grunted again, but whether he agreed or disagreed Harry couldn't tell.

'Come on,' said the first man, as though it was Wilkes who was standing there talking. 'Let's get this lot back before the sun gets to them.'

They carried the fish back into the shadows. Then they were out of sight.

Harry sat back on his heels. It was hard crouching for so long. He looked through the hole again, but there was nothing there. It might just be luck, he thought, to have seen anyone at all. Most of the time there'd be no one there.

He stood and went to the door of the shed.

The chooks had finished with the scraps. Arnie Shwarzenfeather strutted round the edges of the flock as they scratched and pecked and investigated interesting bits of dirt and grass.

Above them the garden shone in the sunlight — the roses great-grandma had planted, and Mum's grevilleas and the tall oak trees that sheltered the lawn. It was hard to think that they hadn't been there back then. It felt like they'd always been there, that everything had always been the same, just like his family had always lived on the farm, and Grandad's farm down the road. Dad and Mum, and Gran and Grandad, and great-grandad and . . .

Even the valley had changed so much, thought Harry. He wondered what the rest of the valley would have looked like in Cissie's time.

Mostly trees, probably, and kangaroo grass that would turn red in autumn, just like it did in the cemetery where the original valley grasses still grew, with little orchids like tiny horse's heads poking through in the spring. There'd be no neat paddocks with well-strained, taut wire fences, no Herefords with their fat round droppings, no houses . . .

There'd be the garrison, of course. It had been down near the river, where they'd get a clear view if the French arrived. The building was still there, about 10 k's out of town. There was a restaurant in it now.

It's funny, thought Harry. He was so used to the restaurant he'd almost forgotten it had once been a garrison. They held wedding receptions and Christmas parties and things like that there, on the green lawns with gardens down to the water.

There probably hadn't been any garden at the garrison in Cissie's day, thought Harry.

The garrison building had been abandoned for years till the gold miners came. It had become a pub, and after that a saddlery, and a funeral parlour, then abandoned for decades before the Stefaniks bought it and turned it into a restaurant.

Maybe Dad and Mum would take him there for dinner one night before he went to boarding school . . . if he went to boarding school . . . He could look at the old walls and imagine Cissie there so long ago.

Harry stretched and stepped out into the sunlight. The chooks glanced at him, then dismissed him. Harry grabbed the empty bucket and walked slowly back up to the house.

What should he do now? Part of him wanted to stay down in the chookhouse, watching the other world through the hole. But part of him needed to anchor himself in his own life for a while, to remind himself that there was another world away from the tragedy of Cissie's. Surely nothing would happen in the other world just for a while . . .

He could do his homework, just like he'd told Mum and Dad he would yesterday. But who could concentrate on homework after what he'd seen?

He could go down to Spike's and go swimming . . . but he didn't want to go down to Spike's. He didn't want other people. He wanted to stay here, near to Cissie, even if he wasn't watching through the hole.

Maybe he *should* do his homework. Then at least he wouldn't have to explain tomorrow why it wasn't done. Then, after lunch, he'd go down to the hole again . . .

Chapter 9

CISSIE'S DECISION

A chook sat on the nest — one of the Australorps, her tiny eyes intelligent in her dark face. She's either Omelette or Chickenpox, thought Harry. The third White Sussex, Wild Thing, refused to lay in the chookhouse. Her eggs were always laid outside, a different nest every few months, as soon as someone found the old nest and took all the eggs.

The chook glared at him, daring him to disturb her till she was finished. 'Don't get all fluffed up,' Harry told her. 'I'm not interested in your egg. Not yet anyway. I'm going to the other side. See?'

He stepped over a pile of fresh droppings under the perch. Please let her be all right now, he thought. Please don't let anything else have happened . . .

It was a clear blue day through the hole, just like it is here, thought Harry. The light looked strangely alike in both places.

But of course it wasn't strange at all. It was valley light, slightly shaded green as the sunlight reflected from the hills, slightly tinged with blue from the eucalyptus oil of the gum tree leaves. The valley caught the light and changed it into something different from sunlight on the tableland, Dad reckoned. Harry supposed it had always been like that.

The sky was blue, and the trees were almost blue as well. Even the creek was blue. Down by the creek Cissie wore her pale blue dress as she watched the waterlily pads shiver in the breeze.

She wasn't crying today, Harry noted happily, but she looked like she had been. Her eyes were red. Her face was very white. She stared at the waterlilies and didn't move.

'Cissie? Cissie girl?'

It was that man from this morning, Harry realised. The quiet one. Wilkes — that was his name.

Cissie glanced up. 'Good afternoon, Sergeant Wilkes,' she said politely.

'I thought I'd find you here, girlie,' said Sergeant

Wilkes in his too-hoarse voice. 'Sitting by yourself again.'

Cissie nodded. Sergeant Wilkes sat on a nearby rock. 'It's good to be by yourself sometimes,' he said. 'It's good to be quiet.'

Neither spoke for a while. Harry wriggled to ease a cramp in his leg. Maybe he should bring a stool down next time. But Mum or Dad might wonder why there was stool in the chook shed.

Sergeant Wilkes rummaged in his pocket and drew out a pipe. He put it in his mouth, but didn't light it, just chewed the end of it thoughtfully. 'Sometimes it's good to talk as well,' he said finally.

'There's nothing to talk about,' said Cissie.

'Well, maybe, maybe not,' said Sergeant Wilkes. 'But sometimes it helps just to get things out into the open, so to speak.'

Cissie raised anguished eyes to Sergeant Wilkes. 'They want to send me back to England!' she cried.

'Well, isn't that a good thing?' asked Sergeant Wilkes. 'It's what most of us want — to go home.'

'But it isn't *my* home. This is my home. It's all I've got, now Mama and Papa —' Her voice broke off.

'But you'll like it back in England,' offered Sergeant Wilkes. He seemed just a bit too emphatic, thought Harry, as though he wasn't sure. 'There's . . . there's all sorts of things at home.'

'Like what?'

'Like . . .' Sergeant Wilkes seemed to search for

something good to say. 'Snow? Wouldn't you like to see snow? A real white Christmas?'

'Snow's cold,' said Cissie. 'I don't like the cold. I couldn't go swimming if there's snow, could I?'

'Well, no,' said Sergeant Wilkes. 'You can toboggan in snow, though. You sit on a tray from the kitchen and down you go . . . your nose gets cold, and your fingers, even in your mittens . . .'

Cissie shrugged, as though the thought of tobogganing held no appeal.

Sergeant Wilkes frowned. 'There are all your cousins,' he offered at last.

'Second cousins once removed,' said Cissie bitterly. 'They don't know me. They don't WANT me.'

'Of course they'll want you.'

'How do you know? They don't even know Papa is dead yet. The mail won't reach them for months and months and then I'll be there before they've had time to say if they really do want me.'

'Of course they'll want you. They're your only living relatives.'

'That doesn't mean they'll want me,' said Cissie. 'Or that I'll want them.'

They were silent for a time.

'Girlie girl, you can't stay here,' said Sergeant Wilkes at last. 'Not now Mrs Sorell's going back. You can travel with her to Sydney on the next supply ship, and then travel back to Dover with her. You can't go all that way by yourself. You have to take this chance to go.'

Cissie shook her head stubbornly. 'I can go on the supply ship by myself. I can travel to England with another family that's sailing back. I don't have to go now.'

'But you can't stay here by yourself. Not without a woman to look after you.'

'Why not? Papa looked after me after Mama died. Why can't I stay here with you and Captain Piper and old Sam and Corporal Johnny...'

'But...' Sergeant Wilkes stopped.

'Just till I hear from my cousins,' Cissie pleaded. 'Just till I know they really want me. What if I go back and they ... and they put me in a foundling asylum or something?'

'They wouldn't do that,' protested Sergeant Wilkes.

'They might!'

'Well, if they did the regiment would have something to say to that,' said Sergeant Wilkes. 'The regiment looks after its own and your Papa was in the regiment. That's what the fund is for, for the widows and orphans, and you're an orphan of the regiment...' his voice trailed away, as though he realised it wasn't tactful to call her an orphan. But Cissie didn't seem to mind at all. She was too intent, thought Harry, too concerned to make him see her way.

'Please?' pleaded Cissie.

'Maybe,' said Sergeant Wilkes tentatively. 'Maybe it'd be possible. But it's not my decision to make, you know. It's Captain Piper's.'

'But you'll ask him?'

Sergeant Wilkes stood up. 'I'll ask him, lass.'

'Now?'

'Yes, now. If he's not busy you understand. I won't disturb him if he's busy.'

'And you'll ask if I can stay till the mail comes from my cousins?'

'It might be a year . . . or even more,' pointed out Sergeant Wilkes. 'The news has to get there, and then get back. But yes. I'll ask him, lass. Are you coming with me or are you waiting here?'

'I'll wait here,' said Cissie. 'You'll come back and tell me what he says?'

'I will at that,' said Sergeant Wilkes. 'If I don't come it'll be because the Captain's busy. You'll come back for your supper, won't you?'

'I promise,' said Cissie.

'That's my good lassie,' agreed Sergeant Wilkes. 'You watch out for snakes too — and don't let those bears go dropping on your head.'

Cissie gave a half giggle. Sergeant Wilkes smiled. 'If you're to stay here you'd have to follow orders.'

'I can follow orders,' promised Cissie.

'Well then,' said Sergeant Wilkes. 'Then I'll be . . .'

'Hey, what's going on?'

Harry started. The voice wasn't coming from the hole. It was here. Harry ducked quickly under the perches towards the door.

'Harry? Harry, what the heck are you doing in there?'

'Spike! I was just . . . I was just collecting the eggs for Mum.'

'What with?' Angie poked her head round the chookhouse door. 'You don't have anything to put the eggs in!'

'I . . . er . . . forgot the container.' Harry tried to position himself between Spike and the hole. 'What are you doing here?'

'Us? We came to go swimming. Remember? We arranged it Friday on the bus. What are *you* doing here?' demanded Spike.

'Me? I live here.' Harry tried to laugh.

'No, duckbrain. Here in the chook shed. You practicing to be a rooster or something? Cockadoodle dooo-oo! We looked everywhere for you. Didn't you hear us yelling?'

'I . . . er, no.' He had been so absorbed in the world inside the hole, Harry realised, that he hadn't heard anything else.

'We asked up at the house. Your mum thought you were in the orchard, but you weren't there. We looked in the shed, then Angie suggested you might be in the chook shed —'

'It was a joke,' put in Angie.

'And you were!' finished Spike.

Harry moved forward slowly. If he could stop them coming in any further they mightn't see the hole. Spike and Angie backed out to give him room.

It was going to be okay. They hadn't seen anything. They . . .

'Hey, you forgot the eggs!' Before he could stop her Angie had darted back into the chookhouse. 'Wow, there are lots of them — your chooks must be laying really well. They . . . What's that?'

'What's what?' asked Harry nonchalantly. 'Hey Angie . . .' he tried to think of some way to lure her out of the chookhouse. 'Er, Angie, come here for a minute . . .'

'No, wait, there's something odd over in the corner. Like something floating!'

'Angie . . . no!'

But it was too late.

There was silence in the chookhouse, then Angie's voice, very soft and puzzled. 'This is what you were doing in here, wasn't it? This is what you were looking at.'

'I . . .' Harry couldn't find words to deny it.

'What's she talking about?' demanded Spike.

'It's . . .' Harry hesitated. It sounded crazy to say it was a hole in time. Besides, he didn't want to tell them. Cissie was *his* discovery. Her world was his discovery. He didn't want to share it or . . .

'Spike, come and look at this.' Angie's voice was full of wonder.

Spike cast Harry a final look, then ducked inside the chookhouse.

Harry followed. There was no help for it now. He'd have to explain.

Chapter 10

DISCOVERED!

It was cooler inside the chookhouse than you'd think, although the sun was overhead. The sprawling passionfruit vine growing over the shed sheltered it. Even so, each breath was thick with heat and chook.

Harry leant against one wall, Spike against the other. Angie still crouched by the time hole, one eye on it, the other on her brother and Harry. She didn't look like she was ever going to leave the hole, thought Harry resentfully. As though she'd claimed it now.

'Why do you think it's a hole in time?' Spike demanded.

'It just makes sense,' said Harry. 'Look at Cissie's clothes.'

'Cissie? Her name's Cissie?' demanded Angie, still intent on the world on the other side.

'Cecilia, I think. Cissie must be a nickname. I told you, I only saw her for the first time on Thursday. I don't know all that much about her. But look at her clothes. They look just like the ones people wear on TV when they're supposed to be in the last century. And the creek too — I bet that's what it used to look like before the goldminers came.'

'But you can't have a hole in *time*,' argued Spike.

'What else could it be? I mean, maybe time just sort of rubs away — like your jeans wear out round the knees. Maybe if one part of time is used too much —'

'That doesn't make sense.'

'Why not? Why can't time wear thin, too? So there's a hole, just a little hole and we can see through it.'

'But how come we can hear her but she can't hear us?'

'I don't know. Maybe because we haven't happened in her time yet, so we don't exist.'

'Oh, that's great. Really great. Crazy,' said Spike.

'I don't think it's so crazy,' said Angie, her eye still to the hole. 'Poor kid. I think it's so sad. I wish there was something we could do to help her. Imagine having both your parents die and in a strange place.'

'It's not strange,' protested Spike. 'She's *here*, remember, only a long time ago.'

'Well, it'd be strange to her,' argued Angie.

'What's happening now?' demanded Harry. 'Buzz off Mr J,' as the rooster tried to push past Harry to the drum that held the laying pellets.

Mr J was a Spangled Hamburg bantam, only half the size of Arnold Schwarzenfeather, except for his tail feathers which always looked twice as large. Midnight Sky, Omelette and Wild Thing mostly followed Mr J, though sometimes they answered Arnie's call, just as the other chooks occasionally followed Mr J.

'Go and peck somewhere else,' ordered Harry. 'There's plenty of beetles outside.'

The rooster strutted off, stretching his spotty neck indignantly. 'What's she doing now?' repeated Harry. He wanted to look too, but there was only room for one, and Angie seemed to have commandeered the hole.

'She's just sitting there.'

'But what does she look like? Happy? Sad?'

'She looks like . . . oh, like she's remembering or something. As though she's there, but somewhere else as well.'

'She had a picnic with her parents there,' said Harry awkwardly. 'That was the first time I saw her.

They looked really happy. Maybe she's remembering that.'

'Maybe,' said Angie. 'Oh, I wish I could speak to her. Send her messages or something to say we're thinking about her. Or a present . . . something she wouldn't have . . . like . . . like ribbons or a book or a fluffy toy dog maybe.'

'How about a video game?' suggested Spike.

'Dope,' said Angie. 'She wouldn't know what to do with it. And you can't have a video game floating about last century. It'd be a, what do you call it? An anachronism. Harry, have you tried poking something through?'

'Only my fingers,' said Harry. 'But you couldn't see them on the other side. They just disappeared. It's like I said — we don't exist yet for her.'

'Poke a stick through,' suggested Spike. 'No, here, how about a feather?'

Angie took it uncertainly. 'She might be scared if she sees a feather floating out of nowhere.'

'She'll just think it fell off a bird,' said Spike. 'Go on, try it.'

Angie slipped the feather through the hole. It disappeared, then reappeared a second later, out the other side of the hole. It fell onto a recent dropping on the floor.

'See, I said it wouldn't work,' said Harry. 'Hey, can I have a look now?'

'Sure,' offered Angie.

Harry took her place under the perch. Sunset gave a muffled squawk at the disturbance and settled even more firmly on her eggs.

Harry peered through the hole. It was just as Angie had described. Cissie was just sitting there on the rock, her arms around her legs. She must have taken her boots off. They sat neatly beside her and a pile of something that might have been long socks or thick stockings as well.

'I don't think she's remembering,' he said slowly. 'I think she's just watching.'

'Watching what?' demanded Spike.

'I don't know. Nothing. Lots of things,' he hesitated. 'I mean, haven't you ever sat down by the creek and just sort of watched things.'

Spike shrugged. 'I suppose,' he admitted. 'Hey, wouldn't it be great if something really exciting happened? I mean like bushrangers attacked the garrison and they had this great gun battle, or the convicts revolted maybe. Have they got any convicts up at the garrison? Or pirates — they could sail up the river, then follow the creek up to bury their chests of loot and we could see where they put it —'

'Not with Cissie there!' protested Angie. 'She might get hurt!'

'Yeah, but . . .' Spike shrugged. 'I mean it's a great idea, looking back into the past and everything. But it's not like anything really interesting's happening. It's just a kid just sitting there. I mean, if the hole

went back to Sydney last century there'd be all sorts
of things — convicts and sailors and fights in pubs
and —'

'I . . .' Harry hesitated. He didn't have the words
to explain to Spike how he felt.

Angie glared at her brother. 'You don't have to
stay if you're bored,' she informed him.

'I'm not bored,' argued Spike. 'I'm just . . . give it
up will you, Angie! I don't suppose everyone else
wants a swim . . . okay, okay, I was just asking.' He
looked at his watch. 'Hey, Angie, if we head back
now, we can still see whatsitsname on TV.'

'But I don't want to . . .' began Angie.

'Come on!' urged Spike. 'Nothing more's
happening here anyway.'

Angie stared at Harry.

He nodded, half eager to see them go. 'The
garrison's ages away. It'd be hours before Sergeant
Wilkes could get back.'

Angie gazed back at the hole. 'Is . . . is it okay if
we come back tomorrow? So we can find out if they
let her stay?'

Harry glanced back through the hole, then back
at Angie.

Part of him wanted to refuse. Cissie was his
discovery. It was his hole into the past. But on the
other hand it'd make it much easier to keep a watch
and find out what happened if there were more of
them to take turns. And it'd be mean to say no.

'You won't tell anyone?' he asked.

Spike blinked. 'I suppose not,' he said. 'Not if you don't want us to. Why not?'

'Because Cissie's private,' flared Angie. 'We don't want lots of people gawking at her. Things are bad enough for her without people peering at her through a hole.'

'Sure, sure,' said Spike hurriedly. 'Don't get in a flap about it. I was only asking. Hey, yuk, I've got chook dust all up my nose. See you tomorrow,' he said to Harry.

'See you,' said Harry. He watched them wander back across the flat. The chooks glanced at them, just in case they carried something good to eat, then turned back to their scratching — Rubinstein under the oak trees, and Midday Snail ripping up Mum's petunias again. Mum'd be mad if she saw her.

'Shoo,' he said half-heartedly to Midday Snail. Midday Snail ignored him. Harry clapped his hands at her. She strutted off without looking back.

Harry walked slowly over to the main shed. There was no point staying at the hole. Cissie might be there for hours, and Mum'd be calling him for dinner. He didn't want her to get suspicious if he always came out of the chook shed when she called.

It was odd the way time changed through the hole. It went at the same speed as the modern world while you were looking through it, but then years could pass when you were away. As though just watching fixed it, somehow. But you couldn't watch it all the time.

The chooks peered at him from their stations about the flat, wondering if he was going to get their wheat.

'Oh, all right,' said Harry.

Harry always gave them their wheat before dinner. Would Mum remember to do it if he went to school next year? he wondered. The chooks would miss their snack.

Arnie Shwarzenfeather gave a short crow at the sound of the lid of the wheat barrel being opened, and O'Neil jumped down from her perch on the truck.

O'Neil was old — eight, maybe, or nine. She was the first chook Harry had ever had of his own. He'd named her after the captain of the football team up in town.

O'Neil didn't lay many eggs anymore — maybe half a dozen eggs in early summer, maybe none at all — and most of the time she seemed to be asleep. But she was a nice chook and the tamest of the lot.

'Here you are, O'Neil,' said Harry. He scattered a handful of wheat just for her before throwing the rest out into the pine needles for the other chooks to scratch around and argue over. They never seemed to notice O'Neil's secret feed of wheat. Or maybe Arnie and Mr J knew all the time, and kept the other chooks away.

The chooks bobbled and scratched like they were run by clockwork: peck and lift and peck and lift . . . chooks were peaceful things, thought Harry. No matter how much fuss there was you always felt calmer when you'd been down with the chooks.

He wondered if Cissie had chooks back at the camp. Did soldiers have hens? Not now, of course — he couldn't imagine an army barracks with chooks. But back then . . .? There'd be no way to get eggs if they didn't have chooks.

How often did the supply boat that Cissie had mentioned come? It must bring flour and meat and tea and coffee. Did they have coffee back then? Probably not. Or cola either. Imagine a world without a can of cola . . . what did they drink then?

Angie might know. She was interested in history and stuff like that.

Angie understood. Spike would keep the secret — he wasn't the sort to go around telling if you asked him not to. But Angie really understood.

The hens had finished the wheat, both the real stuff and the imaginary grains they thought they could see among the pine needles. A couple of them began scratching again, looking for cicada and moth larvae. O'Neil had gone to bed, huddled on the lowest perch next to the far wall. Once she'd been on the top perch, but as she'd aged she'd been pushed down to the second then the third and now the last.

Did chooks mind losing the top position?

wondered Harry. They must, or there wouldn't be all the squawking about who got what position last thing at night.

'Harry! Dinner!'

Harry left the chooks to their scratching. He'd come down and lock them in after dinner, when it was getting dark and they were all inside.

What would Cissie have for dinner, he wondered. Fish maybe (did they have chips back then?), or roast kangaroo . . .

Did people eat tomato sauce in the olden days? Would she eat dinner with all the soldiers? Or did the officers and men eat separately and she ate with one or the other?

What did she do after dinner? Read by candlelight? Play cards? Or did the soldiers go to bed as soon as it got dark, and get up early in the morning.

For a moment he wondered if he should look through the hole after dinner. But it would be dark in the hole by then. Cissie would be back at the garrison. There'd be nothing to be seen at all.

Chapter 11

MONDAY

'Harry!'

'In here!' Harry peered out of the main shed. It was Angie. She wore jeans and an old T-shirt that Spike had outgrown and her riding boots. She was alone.

'Where's Spike?'

'He went fencing with Dad.' She shrugged. 'He says to tell him if anything interesting happens. Hey, I thought you'd be looking at the hole!'

'I was earlier. There's no one there. I just came in here to get some chicken wire. I told Dad I was extending the chook run. It's a good excuse to be down there all the time.'

Angie nodded. 'Mind if I go and look?'

'No, sure. I'll be over there in a minute.'

Harry hauled out the old netting from the back of the shed and considered it. Dad had rolled it up properly so it wasn't tangled, and it still looked in fairly good shape. Good enough for another chook run at least.

Harry dragged it over to the chookhouse, narrowly avoiding Magic Mary, who was hopping from one foot to another in front of the shed.

'You want to go in and lay your egg under the truck again do you?' asked Harry. 'Okay, off you go. I'm finished in there now. But I'm still going to collect it this afternoon, no matter where you lay it.'

Magic Mary ignored him. She disappeared under the truck.

Harry left the roll of wire outside the chookhouse and peered in.

'See anything?' he asked.

Angie shook her head. 'Just a kookaburra. It's sitting right up on top of the big red gum across the creek. And another bird flew right past the hole — it was too close to see what it was.'

Angie looked back through the hole again. 'The creek looked nice back then, didn't it? Sort of peaceful.'

Harry nodded. 'Call me if you see anything,' he

said. 'I'm going to start digging a couple of post holes so it looks like I've done something.'

Angie nodded. 'Need a hand?'

'No, I'm right.'

It was hot digging holes. Harry finished the fourth one and stuck his head back in the chookhouse.

'I'm going down for a swim,' he said. 'Want to come?'

'Didn't bring my bathers.'

'Doesn't matter. Wear your T-shirt. It'll dry soon enough.'

Angie hesitated. 'Okay,' she said finally. 'I don't suppose anything'll happen while we're gone.'

'We can't watch it all the time,' said Harry. 'Not when we're at school or at night. It's just luck really that I've seen all I have.'

Angie nodded. She blinked as she came out into the sunlight. 'Wow. You don't realise how dark it is in there. Don't the chooks mind?'

'Nah, they like it that way. They like to lay someplace dim. Like Magic Mary. She always lays under the truck. And Moonlight's got a nest in the lavender.'

'That's a pretty name,' said Angie.

'Mum chose it,' said Harry. 'When Moonlight was a chick she was sort of pale yellow — a real moonlight colour. She's pure white now though. She's the only Leghorn we've got — I got her egg up at the Show. It was laid by the Champion Hardfeather Fowl. There she was sitting with an egg at the side of the cage, so I asked if I could have it. The bloke said yes, so I put it under a bantam when I got home.'

'The same one who's sitting now?'

'Nah. That's Sunset. She's a really good mother. I've got her on a dozen eggs, even though she's so small. She hatched ten last time. They were all bigger than she was after a couple of months — she looked really silly, as if she'd adopted a mob of baby emus and was trying to teach them how to scratch.'

The rocks around the creek were splashed with sunlight and lichen. The water looked cold. Harry supposed it was cold in Cissie's day, too.

He dived in quickly to get his body used to the chill, then surfaced and floated through the ripples where the creek fell in a smooth cascade into the swimming hole. You could slide down the cascade for hours when the water was a bit deeper, till your legs were red and your bum ached with the cold.

Harry breathed in the scent of water and rotting casuarina needles, of ribwort and watercress and stonewort. One of his earliest memories was of the creek. Mum brought him down here when he was still toddling to splash in the shallows and try to chase the dragonflies at the edges of the water. It hurt to imagine the creek still flowing here, the ripples of water and sunlight, while he was away at school . . .

'Harry?'

'Mmmm?'

'What were Cissie's parents like?'

Harry hesitated. 'Nice, I think. I only saw them all together once. And I didn't really see them then — just Cissie. But they sounded nice.'

Angie sighed. 'I hope the soldiers let her stay. It'll be horrible if they don't.'

'It's all already happened,' Harry pointed out.

'I know. But it doesn't seem like it.' Angie hauled herself up onto a rock. 'I'm going back. You coming?'

Harry nodded.

The chook shed smelt even more strongly of chook as the day became hotter. At least half a dozen hens had laid in their absence, Harry noted. They must have been crossing their legs till they left.

'I'll watch for a while if you like,' offered Harry.

'It'd be better if I watch,' said Angie. 'Then you can be working on the chook run if your parents come down and check. I promise I'll call you as soon as anything happens.'

If anything happens, thought Harry. Maybe Cissie has already gone.

But he didn't say it aloud.

Chapter 12

Looking for Cissie

The shadows lengthened.

White Ice, the Light Sussex, peered into the chookhouse and saw Angie. She considered for a moment, her small pale head on one side, her black neck twisted, then hopped into the far right nesting box.

Twenty minutes later Harry heard her call. *Pruck pruck opruck pruck opruck pruck pruck . . .*

'Dopey birds,' sighed Angie. 'No, there's nothing happening. I just wanted to stretch for a moment and get out of the chook dust. Why do they call like that anyway? Everyone knows they've laid an egg and can come and take it.'

'It's to signal to the rooster,' said Harry. 'When he hears them cluck he knows to look round and make sure it is safe for them to get back to him and the other chooks.' He glanced at his watch. 'What time do you have to be back?'

'Soon,' said Angie. 'I haven't finished my homework. I've still got all those maths problems. Surely something must have happened by now.'

'Maybe we've missed it. While we were down at the creek . . . or before breakfast.'

'Or they've sent her home. They *can't* have sent her home. We'd never see her again. We'd never know . . .' She stopped, as though embarrassed by her own vehemence. 'I'd better get home myself. What about tomorrow?'

'I'll look before I go to school,' said Harry. 'Damn. I can't after school though — I've got basketball practice and Mum's picking me up. It'll be five at the earliest before we get home.'

'Would you like me to come down and check?' asked Angie hesitantly.

'Would you? That'd be great. I'll tell Mum we're doing a project together or something.'

'Okay. Just so I know what I'm supposed to be doing here. When are Sunset's eggs going to hatch?'

'About a week,' said Harry. 'It's been fourteen, no fifteen days so far.'

'If anyone asks what I'm doing in the chookhouse I'll say I'm checking the eggs,' said Angie. 'And waiting for you of course.' She hesitated. 'Maybe I'll look just one more time,' she said. She slipped inside the chookhouse and pressed her eyes to the hole.

'Harry!'

'What? What is it?'

'She's there! She's back again!' Angie's face was glowing. 'Oh Harry, they did let her stay!'

Chapter 13

CISSIE RETURNS

Cissie was older. But not much taller, thought Harry, as he crouched under the perches with Angie.

If they sort of sat opposite each other with their eyes at an angle, they could both get their eyes close enough to the hole to see inside at the same time.

Cissie was still dressed much the same as before. But her face looked . . . different somehow, he decided. It was almost the face of the woman she would become.

She was sitting on her rock. The same rock she

had sat on the first time Harry saw her, and the last. She was reading aloud from a book in her lap, a solid sort of book, with a leather cover stained at one side.

Sergeant Wilkes leant against a flat-trunked gum on the bank opposite. He held a fishing line. Or at least that's what Harry supposed it was. It was just a stick and a piece of thread dropping into the water.

'That was a nice one,' said Sergeant Wilkes in his croaking voice.

He looked older too, thought Harry, much older than Grandad now. The hair had shrunk from his head like grass in a drought. 'A very nice one indeed. Not that I understood it, mind you. But it was nice the way you read it.'

Cissie's face was laughing, so different from the girl Harry had seen just a few days before.

'You didn't even listen,' she accused. 'Your eyes were shut.'

'I can listen with me eyes shut,' said Sergeant Wilkes amiably. 'Read me another then.'

Cissie looked down at her book again. 'To Daffodils,' she read. 'It's by Robert Herrick. Captain Piper says Herrick was a very famous poet.'

'He's dead then?'

Cissie hesitated. 'I think all poets are dead,' she said. 'All the good ones. All the ones in Captain Piper's book are dead anyway.' She cleared her throat.

'Fair daffodils, we weep to see
You haste away so soon:
As yet the early rising Sun
Has not attain'd his noon.
Stay, Stay,
Until the hasting day
has run
But to the evensong
and, having pray'd together, we
Will go along with you
We have as short a time to stay as you;
We have as short a spring;
As quick a growth to meet decay
as you, or anything.
We die,
as your hours do, and dry
Away
Like to the summer's rain,
Or as the pearls of morning dew.
Ne'er to be found again.'

Her voice grew silent.

'Ah, that's a sad one,' said Sergeant Wilkes at last. 'Things growing, changing, passing. But flowers come again. Maybe that poet of the Captain's forgot about that!'

Sergeant Wilkes drew up the string, examined it, then reached beside him for a gobbet of meat. He tied it back onto the string and threw it in.

'He must be trying to catch an eel,' whispered Angie. 'There's no hook on his line for fish.'

Harry nodded. There was no need to whisper, of course. Neither Cissie nor Sergeant Wilkes could hear them. But it seemed wrong to speak aloud just the same.

'Sergeant Wilkes?'

'Yes, lass?'

'What are daffodils like?'

Sergeant Wilkes looked nonplussed. 'Well, they're flowers, lass. Yellow flowers. Like any flowers I suppose.'

'Like wattle?'

'Well no. Not like that. They stick out of the ground on a straight stem, one at a time.'

'They'd look silly!'

'Well they don't, lass, and that's a fact. They look right beautiful. You ask Captain Piper about them. He'll tell you right enough. He's the one with all the learning.'

Cissie nodded. She looked down at her book, then looked back at Sergeant Wilkes. 'Has anyone ever written a poem about wattle?'

Sergeant Wilkes looked startled. 'Not that I know of, lass. You'd best ask Captain Piper about that as well. But I don't suppose they have. Wattle doesn't grow back home where the poets were. Too cold.'

'I bet wattle's prettier than any daffodils,' said Cissie stubbornly.

Wilkes chuckled. 'Well, you might be right at that. But don't let Captain Piper or Lieutenant Carstairs hear you say it. Lieutenant Carstairs has a whole wood of daffodils right by his home in Surrey. He talks about them every spring. You'll see daffodils for yourself one day, lass. Then you'll see why they write poems about them.'

'I'll still like wattle best,' said Cissie obstinately. 'Maybe I'll write a poem about wattle, if no one else has. "Fair wattle branch that waves about the sky . . ." What rhymes with sky, Sergeant Wilkes?'

'Ah, no, that's not a question you should be asking me neither,' said Sergeant Wilkes. He stretched. 'I've been sitting in one place long enough. Me bones are aching. Come on. They're not biting today, or maybe the meat's too fresh for them to fancy.'

Cissie nodded. 'Fly,' she said.

'What's that lass?'

'Fly. It rhymes with sky. And high, and lie . . . "Fair wattle branch that waves about the sky, There against the blue you lie, Showing the . . . bees, maybe . . . the bees . . . or laughing jackasses. . . no, bees sounds better. . . Showing the bees then how to fly . . ."'

'Then you'd better run back and write it down before you go forgetting it,' said Sergeant Wilkes. 'I bet it'll be a grand poem. Don't you go waiting for me, lass. I'll come as fast as my bones can carry me and no faster.'

Cissie clasped her book and leapt across the rock. Suddenly she was gone. Her voice floated back, too indistinct to hear what she was saying, then Sergeant Wilkes was gone as well.

There was silence in the chookhouse. Outside, Arnie Shwarzenfeather yodelled to his flock. Showing them a patch of grass seed, thought Harry, or just keeping them together. The dust wove and quivered in the sun streaks that came through the door.

'It wasn't very good,' said Harry at last. He felt disloyal, but he had to say something.

'What wasn't?'

'Cissie's poem. It wasn't very good.'

'It was her first poem,' said Angie defensively. 'I bet she gets better at it later on.'

Harry nodded. He didn't want to argue. 'You'll check tomorrow after school?'

'I said I would,' said Angie. She seemed uncertain too, thought Harry, as though neither knew quite what to say. Nothing really seemed adequate.

Looking through the hole wasn't like watching TV or a video. It was real life. They were the watchers who could offer neither sympathy nor help. Or even a rhyme for sky, thought Harry.

Try, cry, goodbye . . .

'See you tomorrow,' said Harry finally.

Angie nodded without speaking. Harry watched her cross the flat and go down the path to home.

Chapter 14

NEXT WEEK

The school bus wound down the spaghetti road, clattering over the bridge at Three Sheep Creek, bouncing over the ruts the Council grader flattened once a year and that came back as soon as it rained and the water washed across the road.

'Coming swimming?' asked Spike.

Harry shook his head. 'I'm going down to the chookhouse,' he said.

Spike blinked at him. 'You're always down the chookhouse these days. Doesn't it get sort of boring?' he demanded.

Harry shrugged. It wasn't boring. It was compelling, more and more each day, as though he *had* to know what happened next, as though there was something that made him look.

'Anything new happened this week?' asked Spike.

Harry glanced behind, but no one was listening. Trudi and Alice were whispering secrets and Sam was just staring out the window. 'Didn't Angie tell you?' asked Harry.

Spike shrugged. 'Didn't ask,' he said. 'She'd just say, Why don't you come down and see for yourself?, in a silly sort of voice . . . You know what sisters are like.'

Harry nodded, though he didn't, not having a sister. 'We've only seen her twice this week,' he said slowly. 'The first time Angie got there just as Cissie was leaving. And the second time Cissie was reading by herself.'

'Like I said. Boring,' said Spike. 'Just sitting in a chookhouse watching a kid sit on a rock. Maybe something will happen soon. Hey, wouldn't it be great if you saw bushrangers? You could see where they put their treasure then we could go and dig it up.'

'I don't think there were bushrangers around much then,' said Harry. 'Bushrangers were later.'

'Well, something interesting,' said Spike. 'Hey, have you decided about next year yet?'

'No,' said Harry shortly.

'I'd go like a shot,' said Spike. 'Anything to get away from Bradley's Bluff. I mean at least things *happen* down in Sydney. You know Angie's applied for a scholarship at St Helen's?'

'No,' said Harry startled. 'She didn't say anything about it.'

'I reckon she'll get it,' said Spike. 'She's pretty bright. But then she's interested . . . hey, that means if you decide to go down to Sydney she'll be able to tell you all the news. I won't have to write two letters. The schools are pretty close, aren't they?'

'Dunno,' said Harry.

'I reckon it'd be great to go,' said Spike.

The bus lumbered round a bend. Below, the river bed gleamed like it had soaked up all the sun. The last of summer's water trickled through deep ruts carved in the sand.

Harry was silent.

Chapter 15

DANIEL

'Harry! Is that you?'

'Yeah, it's me.' Harry dumped his school bag on the verandah.

'Take your boots off before you come inside,' said Mum automatically.

'Mum, they're school shoes. Not boots. They haven't been anywhere dirty.'

'They're dirty enough,' said Mum. 'No shoes inside. There's frozen fruit salad in the freezer if you want some.'

'Great. I'll take some down with me.'

'Down to the chook shed again?'

Harry nodded.

'You're down there every afternoon and the new run is hardly started.' Mum grinned at him. 'I bet I know what you're really doing down there.'

Harry froze. 'What?'

'Just watching your chooks. My dad was the same. When he was appointed someplace new the first thing he'd unpack would be his hens. It used to drive my mother demented sometimes. She'd be unpacking all the kid's things and he'd be down checking out the back shed or whatever was there to put his chooks in . . . And every Sunday when he came back from the service they'd be waiting for him, all lined up. He always gave them a special lot of wheat at Sunday lunchtime. He swore they could count to seven and knew just when Sunday was.'

'Probably just heard the music in Church and thought "wheat",' said Harry.

'Probably,' said Mum. 'You know, it's funny. We moved six times when I was a kid. And here I am married to a man whose family has lived in the one spot for six generations.'

And I'm the seventh, thought Harry. But he didn't say it aloud. Mum and Dad never pressured him about taking over the farm. Never even said 'When you do ag science at high school . . .' If he wanted to be an accountant or a computer scientist they wouldn't argue. But he knew they hoped he'd find some way to keep the farm no matter what else he decided to do.

The chook shed shimmered in the heat, even under its blanket of passionfruit. He'd scraped out all the muck and put down fresh hay on Tuesday (he'd seen Angie wrinkle her nose on Monday). The chooks kept scratching it over, looking for seeds, and so kept covering their droppings with the hay, too. The shed still smelt more like dried grass than chook.

Harry stepped inside. All the eggs were in the lefthand box today, as though the chooks had had a conference that morning and decided, It's the left one today, girls.

The hole was a bright white light in the darkness. It must be summer there too, thought Harry. When it was winter on the other side the hole was softer, dimmer. He crouched down and pressed his eyes to it.

Someone was there! Someone new! Not Cissie, not Sergeant Wilkes, not any of the people he'd seen before.

This was a boy, about his age or a few years older. He wore a shirt and trousers, sort of baggy, but not so different from what you'd wear today, and heavy boots.

The boy knelt by the creek scooping its water into his mouth. A stained sack drooped behind him. A horse whinnied softly in the background, but it was too far to the side to see.

'Who are you?'

Harry started. It was Cissie's voice. The hole showed so little of its world, he hadn't seen her approach and still couldn't see where she was. She must be standing just downstream.

The boy jumped. He gulped water the wrong way, so he choked, and stood up coughing. 'What the . . . what are you doing creeping up on me like that? I might have drowned meself in fright.'

Cissie's voice was unsympathetic. 'Only if you'd been fool enough to stick your head in the pool. Who are you?' she repeated.

'Who wants to know?'

'I do.'

The boy shrugged. 'Daniel then.'

'Daniel what?'

'Who gave you the right to ask the questions?'

'You can ask too if you like.' Cissie stepped forward, closer to the boy. Harry could see her clearly now.

'I don't need to ask questions,' said the boy smugly. 'I know who you are and all anyway.'

'Who am I then?'

'You're the girl who lives at the garrison with the soldiers. Captain Piper told my Da all about you.'

'Oh!' Cissie sat on the bank and hugged her knees. 'That's who you are then! The new people who've settled down the river. Captain Piper said you'd all come up to join your father.'

'Who did you think I was then?'

Cissie wrinkled her nose. 'How was I to know? An escaped convict maybe.'

'Do I look like an escaped convict?'

Cissie looked him up and down. 'You might be.'

'Well, I wouldn't be wearing my best clothes to go honeying, would I?' demanded the boy, exasperated.

'Is that what you've been doing? Getting honey?'

The boy nodded. 'One of the black women down the river told my ma about a hive along the creek up this way. The dray overturned when we crossed a river — only a week out from Sydney, too — and all the sugar got wet and dissolved away, and then the ants got in the treacle. It's been weeks since Ma had any sweetening and when she heard about the honey . . .'

'Weren't you afraid they'd sting you?' asked Cissie admiringly.

'Nah, these is native bees. Native bees don't sting.'

'How do you know?'

'The black women said. They know everything, the black women do. The bees didn't sting me, so it must be true. Besides, it'd've been worth it for the honey.' The boy grinned again. 'And I got something a touch better than honey.'

'What?' demanded Cissie.

'A swarm! A swarm of bees! They just dropped into my sack, easy as you please.' The boy gestured to the sack on the ground.

'They're in there? Can I see them? Please!'

'Course not. They might fly away. Or, maybe if they get angry they sting.'

'Could I just see the honey then?' Cissie hesitated. 'I've never seen honey.'

'Never!'

'Not that I remember. Maybe I did back in Sydney or back in England — but I was too young then to remember anything . . . or not much anyway. Not honey. I've read about it though. I've read a lot. Captain Piper's got two whole chests of books, and Mama and Papa had some as well . . . Can I see it? Please?'

The boy hesitated, then vanished in the direction of the horse whinny. He was back a few seconds later. He held out a slightly grubby hand. 'You can taste it if you like,' he offered.

'Really? Your ma won't be angry?'

'There's plenty there,' reassured Daniel. 'It was a whole tree full. They're not like bees back home. I've never seen a hive so big before.'

'Did you keep bees back home?'

'My grandfather did. Twenty skeps out the back, and more sometimes. He made mead too, but they never let me taste it,' said the boy regretfully.

'What's mead?'

'It's a drink. Honey and spring water. It's got to be spring water mind, that's what grandfather said. And yeast. Some people add herbs as well, but grandfather says they spoil the taste. Then you let it brew and that's the mead. Like beer maybe, but better. Least that's what grandfather said.' Daniel held his hand out to her again. 'Here, take it.'

Cissie lifted the lump from the boy's hand. It looked sticky, and sort of shiny. It must be honeycomb, Harry realised, not like the honey that came in jars.

Cissie tasted it. 'It's . . . it's strange.'

'But good,' asked Daniel anxiously.

'Good,' agreed Cissie. She tasted it again.

'I'd give you some to take home,' said the boy regretfully. 'But I did promise Ma.'

'No, please,' said Cissie quickly. 'I wouldn't want to take your honey. Maybe . . . maybe you'll be this way again though. You could show me the tree. Then I could get some for myself.'

'I will if I can,' said Daniel. 'But I can't tell you when. It took me and Mabel half the day to ride here, and it'll be the rest of the day to get back, and the roof's still not secure on the house and there are fences to build . . .'

'I understand,' said Cissie softly.

'Maybe you could come our way sometime? It's a grand spot we've got by the river. The most beautiful place you'll ever see!'

Cissie was silent for a moment. 'I like the creek,' she said finally. 'It's sort of mine. I don't think I'll ever see a place more beautiful than this.'

'But this is a creek, not a river! A river's much more grand.'

'This is my place,' said Cissie stubbornly. 'I think it's lovely.'

The boy looked round, as though seeing the cascades, the waterlilies, the gentle grass for the first time. 'Well, it's a beautiful place, too,' he agreed. 'Do you think you can come? One of the soldiers will bring you surely if you ask?'

'I will if I can,' said Cissie. She hesitated. 'It's nice to have someone to talk to. Someone who isn't a soldier. I mean I love them all, but . . . do you have any sisters?' she asked hopefully.

'Three,' said Daniel cheerfully. 'All younger than me and all the worst nuisances you've seen in all your born days. Sarah's the oldest. A a bit younger than you, I think. Then there's Bet and Laura, and two brothers, too, Benjamin and Charlie. Charlie's eight years old and Ben is seven. And we've dogs — a pair of them — and a dozen hens and twenty-seven head of cattle.'

'I've got a pet bear,' said Cissie wistfully. 'It eats gum leaves. But it sleeps most of the day. I'd like to see dogs.'

'You *must* get them to bring you down!' urged Daniel.

'I will,' said Cissie. 'I will.'

The horse whinnied and they walked away. Harry waited, but neither came again.

Chapter 16

HEART'S PLACE

White Ice had laid an egg and wanted to proclaim it to the world. Sky Maze leapt up onto the box beside her, prepared to lay on top of her if she wouldn't move. White Ice squeaked and flapped down to the floor.

'I wish I'd seen them,' said Angie. It was Saturday morning. Angie had brought three pots of jam — her mum had been cooking up the last of the apricots — and her homework to fill in time while Harry was watching through the hole.

'I wish you'd seen them,' said Harry. It was the truth. Some time in the past week he'd stopped feeling that Angie was an interloper. Cissie was hers now, as well as his.

Angie peered down at the hole again, and shook her head. 'Still nothing,' she said. 'You know, it's funny. It's almost as though nothing happens till we're watching.'

'Except we don't know what's happened that we haven't seen,' said Harry practically. 'I mean all sorts of things might have happened. Cissie might have been bitten by an eel or Sergeant Wilkes might have been carried off by a wedgetailed eagle.' He grinned as Angie giggled. 'Cissie must have been here lots of times when we haven't seen her. It's her favourite spot — her special place, she said.'

'I know. It's just . . . I just feel we haven't really missed anything. But you're right. Who knows what we haven't seen?' She bent down to the hole again. 'Still nothing happening. Feel like a swim? I brought my bathers this time.'

'Okay.'

'I'll meet you down there after I get changed.'

'What, here!' Harry was startled. 'You can't get changed in a chook shed!'

'Why not? The chooks don't mind. They're used to me. I've spent enough time in here in the past week. Go on. I promise I won't disturb your chooks.'

The creek was cold, as though it had searched for all the chill within the rocks and gathered it together in the swimming hole. You could sort of smell the rocks, thought Harry, as he floated on his back. Hot rocks on the top and cold soil and rocks below. Rocks smoothed by a thousand floods, pink rocks, white rocks, grey rocks, rocks and water, rocks and sun. Clouds spilled lazily out from behind the hills and floated slowly along the sky.

Angie slid into the water behind him and stroked slowly out to the rock in the middle of the swimming hole, just submerged below the water. She held onto it with both arms, idly kicking to keep herself horizontal. 'You know it's funny,' she said, after a while.

'What's funny?' Harry still watched the clouds.

'When you first slide in you think your toes will drop off with cold. Then after a while your body sort of gets used to it. You know . . .'

'Yeah.' Harry knew.

'Will you miss all this when you go away?' asked Angie a few minutes later.

Harry rolled over. The spell was broken.

'I don't know if I am going,' he said shortly.

'But Spike said . . .'

'I don't care what Spike said. I haven't made up my mind.'

'It's a good school,' said Angie slowly.

'Yeah.'

'But I suppose you'll get homesick. I will I bet if I get into St Helen's.'

'It's not that.' Suddenly everything seemed clear,

clear as the swimming hole and just as cold. 'I . . . I'm afraid I *won't* get homesick. That I won't miss this place.'

'But . . .'

'Everyone says how great the school is. How much fun you have down in the city. All the other kids, all the things you can't study here. I'm afraid I'll like it too much. That when I come home I won't love it any more. And I *have* to love this place. It's who I am . . . and if I change I don't know who I'll be . . .'

Angie was silent.

'Sorry,' said Harry at last. 'That sounded dumb.'

'No, it didn't,' said Angie. 'I understand, I think.'

A goshawk swooped above them suddenly, its shadow flickering across the pool. It seemed about to grab a fish beneath the water; then saw the children, and twisted up and through the trees instead.

'Come on,' said Harry. 'I'll race you to the other end.'

Chapter 17

DECISION

The end came unexpectedly.

The day was cool, the mist hanging above the hilltops seeping down in an almost imperceptible wet haze. The chooks ruffled down in dust baths as though seeking the warmth stored in the soil, or pecked about the stones in Mum's rockery at the edge of the garden.

They'd seen Cissie twice during the week. Both times she'd been reading. Once, a book, thick with a red cover, but held away from them so they couldn't see it's title, and the other time a letter. Or it had looked like a letter. As Angie had pointed out it might just have been lessons she was supposed to learn, or poems, if she still tried her hand at poetry.

There wasn't really much chance she'd be there today, thought Harry, watching Wild Thing being chased by Hazelnut around the flat. Wild Thing had a beetle and Hazelnut wanted it . . . Harry stepped inside the chook shed and crossed over to the hole.

There was no mist in the world within the hole. The sky was clear, the tree trunks dappled brown and red as though there'd recently been rain.

As Harry watched, Cissie stepped into sight. She wore a bonnet, pale straw with ribbons hanging on each side. She looked no older than she had the last time he'd seen her.

Cissie stepped silently onto her rock and sat down. She looked at the pool, at the trees and the sky. She spoke to the face, the gnarled face of bark and ancient sap, on the trunk of the red gum tree that leant across the bank.

'I've come to say goodbye,' she said. She trailed her hand across the water. The waterlilies bobbed in the ripples. She looked up at the tree again.

'I know it's silly saying goodbye to a tree, and to the creek and to the wind. But I've got to say goodbye to someone. They're all packing and seeing to their uniforms and no one has time to take me down to the farm, so I can't say goodbye to Dan and the others. I don't even think they know yet that the garrison is being withdrawn. The boat only came last night.'

She paused again and shut her eyes. For a moment Harry was afraid she'd say the rest of the goodbye in her mind, but after a moment she opened her eyes and spoke again.

'I'll miss you so much,' she said. 'You don't know how I'll miss you. They don't understand, back at the garrison. They don't understand how you can love a place so much it's part of you. They say I have to go home, now that the regiment has to leave here. England isn't home. This is my home, but no one understands.

'They think I should be happy to go. I'll see snow and daffodils and live in a nice house instead of barracks. They think now my cousins have written and say they want me I shouldn't be afraid.

'I'm not afraid. I'm not afraid of anything! But you are all I've got — all I've had of my own for so many years. Why is it so silly to love a place as you'd love a person? If I leave you it'll be as though my heart is wrenched right out of me!'

Was she going to cry? wondered Harry. But her eyes were dry and bright. It was as though she didn't want to waste her last time here with tears. Tears might blur the world, and she wanted every memory to be clear.

'I wanted to beg them to let me stay, stay with Dan's family, but of course I can't. I haven't any money to pay them for my keep and the farm's not paying yet. They've got too many children of their own to take another.

'If I could stay with a family in Sydney maybe it mightn't be so foreign, so strange . . . or even in school there, then one day, somehow, I might get back here . . . but there aren't any schools for girls in Sydney, or not the sort they'd be prepared to leave me in, and no money anyway . . .

'I didn't say anything. They've been so kind. None of them my family, but all of them have made me theirs. They're all so happy at their recall. They'll see their wives and families, the places they love, where they grew up. The bluebell wood, the shaggy ponies, old Sam's public house — the tiniest in England, Captain Piper says — badger hunting, chestnuts . . . all the things that they remember.

'Let them think that I'm happy to go back, that I'll be glad to be living with my cousins. That's the best way that I can thank them now.'

There was another pause.

'Goodbye,' she said.

Wild Thing had eaten her beetle. Smokin' Joe and Sky Maze hesitated at the door, then trotted in to peck at the chicken pellets in the feeder on the wall.

Harry walked across the flat and up the stairs. The house was empty. Dad was off at a sale somewhere, and Mum had gone as well.

The phone was in the kitchen. Harry picked the

receiver up. It felt cold to his touch. He dialled the number carefully — 8, 6, 3 ...

'Mrs Lucas? It's Harry. Could I speak to Angie please?'

'Angie, it's me. Something's happened. Something terrible has happened. Do you think you could come down?'

Chapter 18

GONE!

'But she can't have gone!' cried Angie, for what seemed the hundredth time. 'They must have realised that she was upset, even if she wasn't going to tell them. They must have noticed *something* wrong. They *must* have let her stay.'

'Stay where?'

'At that boy's place. Daniel's. Or even down in Sydney.'

'She had no money.'

'One of them could have paid for her.'

'Why should they? They weren't related to her.'

'But she loved them! She must have loved them! Sergeant Wilkes and Captain Piper and all the others — they must have loved her back.'

'Maybe they did,' said Harry slowly. 'Maybe none of them had enough money to pay for a kid to stay in Australia. I don't suppose they were paid a lot back then and they'd have families to support, back in England. And they'd have said to each other, "Well, she has people who'll look after her. Nice people more than likely." Cissie said they had a big house. They had more money probably than anyone at the garrison. The soldiers might have thought she'd be homesick for a while, but once she had other kids for company and proper lessons, a governess maybe . . .' Harry's voice trailed off.

'Then she'd forget,' finished Angie.

Harry nodded.

'I don't think she'd forget,' declared Angie. 'I think this place was too much part of her. I think she'd remember. And I don't think she left. She can't have! I think she would have found some way to stay.'

'But how?'

'I don't know. But we have to keep on looking. We have to find out, Harry. We can't stop now. We have to see.'

'But what if there's nothing! What if we look for years and never see anything at all.'

'I . . .' Angie stopped. 'Harry. We're all she has.

Even if she doesn't know about us — even if she never will. We can't abandon her. We have to be here for her — just so there's someone waiting ...'

'But it can't make any difference now!' cried Harry. 'It's lost. It's gone.'

'It hasn't gone!' said Angie passionately. 'It's still there through that hole. Even if we can't see it! It's the past and the past is still here with us, all the time.'

'But you can't change the past!' yelled Harry.

'But, but, but ... you sound like a chook,' flared Angie. 'Harry — do you *want* to leave her? Do you *want* to stop watching?'

'No,' said Harry.

Suddenly all his anger was gone. He wasn't angry at Angie anyway. He was angry at ... at nothing. At everything. At the past for being so untouchable, at school next year and at the future for being so unknowable. Angry at himself, maybe, for being powerless when someone he cared about was being hurt, so very far away.

'You're right,' he said at last. 'We'll keep on watching.'

Chapter 19

SEARCHING FOR CISSIE

'Angie?' Harry peered through the chookhouse door. 'I brought you down some cordial. It's pineapple. I hope that's okay.'

Angie lifted her eyes from the hole. It seemed to pulse today, dark and light and dark again. Harry wondered if there was wind on the other side, blowing the clouds across the sun.

'Thanks,' said Angie. 'It's okay. I like pineapple.' She crawled out underneath the perch and took the glass.

'See anything?'

Angie shook her head. 'I'd have called you if I had. Just a fish jumping at some insects. And there was a black snake, too. But not Cissie. Not people at all.'

That's all they'd seen all week, thought Harry. Wallabies . . . and once a kookaburra laughing at the wind. But never Cissie, or anything that might tell them where she'd gone.

'They must have all left,' said Harry slowly. 'The garrison withdrew. That was the last time she was able to come to the creek . . .'

'But there must be someone left!' cried Angie.

Harry shook his head. 'My great-something-grandad took up this place in the 1840s, and there wasn't anyone here then. Not even any Aboriginal people. They'd all got sick or something, I can't remember what. But I remember Gran saying it was years before they started to come back down here again.'

Harry crouched down with his back against the doorjamb.

'There's no point us keeping watch anymore,' he said reluctantly. 'We just have to face it. We might watch the hole for twenty years and not see anyone.'

'But time doesn't pass in the hole like it does here!' protested Angie. '*Years* have gone by there since you first saw Cissie. Maybe years have passed there now.'

Years without Cissie, thought Harry forlornly. He shook his head. 'She's not coming back no matter how long we look. No one is coming back.'

'But we can't just leave her like this!' cried Angie.

'We've got no choice,' said Harry. 'She's gone, Angie. And no matter how long we look we won't find her.'

'It's like . . . it's like we're abandoning her!'

'We're not abandoning her, Angie. We'll still think of her — hope for her. But we just have to face it — no matter how hard we hope, how much we look through the hole, we're never going to know what happened to her.'

'I don't believe that,' persisted Angie. 'It must be somewhere. In a history book . . .'

'Who'd put a kid like Cissie in a history book. History's all wars and exploration . . .'

'But there must be some way we can find out what happened to her. Maybe, maybe there's records down in Sydney. You know, of passengers on boats and things. We could look up the passenger lists and see if she left.'

'But we don't know what year!'

'We can find out! They must know at the museum when the garrison was withdrawn — that'll give us the year — then if we check all the ships.'

'But how?' asked Harry.

'I don't know! But someone must know how to

do it. Even if we have to go down to Sydney . . . we can't just leave her there, Harry. Not all alone.'

'She's been alone for over a hundred years,' said Harry quietly. 'She never knew we'd been watching her. She never knew we cared about her . . .'

'She must have known,' said Angie stubbornly. 'She must have felt it. I bet that's why she kept coming back here, to the spot where we saw her. Because she sensed there was someone there who cared about her, who loved her, who cared what happened to her.'

'Don't cry,' said Harry finally. He wondered if he should put his arm round her, but he was too embarrassed.

'I'm not. It's just dusty in here, that's all.' Angie rubbed her eyes roughly with the back of her hand, leaving grey smudges across her cheeks. 'I'll ask Mum if I can go and stay with Aunt Cassie down in Sydney next holidays. She did history at the Uni. She might know how to find out things like that.'

'Okay,' said Harry. After all, she might just find something out. Maybe there *would* be a record of Cissie.

'We could write to the regiment in England, too,' he offered, trying to smile. 'Maybe it's still going on. I mean, don't they have regimental histories and things like that? Maybe there's someone in England who knows.'

'Sure,' said Angie stubbornly. 'There are lots of things we can try.'

She didn't meet his eyes.

She knows it's no use, thought Harry. Cissie was just a kid over a hundred years ago.

No one would keep records of a kid.

Cissie had vanished. They would never know where she had gone.

Chapter 20

FINAL CLUE

The paddocks shimmered on either side as the bus wound down the spaghetti road. Spike grabbed his bag as the bus slowed down, then tossed Angie hers. She glanced at Harry and hesitated.

'Should I come up this afternoon?' she asked.

Harry shrugged. 'You can if you like,' he said. 'I mean there's not much point. Not now.'

'But you'll check if there's anyone through the ...' she broke off as Spike nudged her. He gestured at Mac, and shook his head.

'But you'll look,' pleaded Angie.

'Of course I'll look,' said Harry. 'I'll ring you if I see anything.'

He watched Spike and Angie get off the bus and start the walk up the hill to their house. Angie stopped and looked back. Her face was intent, her eyes sombre. As though she was willing him to keep on looking, to see something, to find Cissie once again.

But Cissie was gone.

The bus swung out into the road again. Round one corner, round the next. It pulled up beside the old diesel drum that Dad had painted red and white, that they used as a mailbox.

'Thanks Mac,' said Harry.

'Have a good weekend,' said Mac. 'Hey, by the way, what was Angie talking about back there? Look at what?'

'Oh, just one of the chooks,' said Harry glibly. 'Old Sunset. She hatched some chickens last week. We think we might finally have got that Araucana–Australorp cross. Angie was just reminding me to check on them.'

'Well, good luck with them,' said Mac. The bus doors closed with a whoosh.

Harry picked up the mail, absently avoiding the huntsman spider in the corner. The huntsman lived on flies and moths and was used to hands appearing in its home and grabbing letters out, but it just might bite if someone grabbed it by mistake.

The track was hot. Dust puffed round his ankles with each step. It was cooler in the shade of the hedge nearer the house, tall and dusty green on either side of the path. Dad trimmed it back every year, otherwise it'd grow as tall as the verandah, Dad said. It was so thick you could wriggle inside and no one would see you. Harry had tried it lots of times when he was small.

It was even cooler near the house. Mum had turned on the sprinkler on the grass. The breeze gusted through it, cool breaths among the heat. The oak trees' shade looked almost dark blue over the lawn.

Harry glanced down towards the chookhouse. There was no sign of the chooks. They'd be resting under the lavender bushes or in the shade by the creek, their feathers fluffed up to insulate them.

There was no point in going down to the chookhouse. He could collect the eggs when it grew cooler, and check on Sunset's chickens. There was no point looking at the hole in the chookhouse now. There'd be nothing to see. Just the creek from last century wandering through the waterlilies; just Cissie's tree and the sky that looked the same no matter what century you were in.

Harry hesitated. It was no use. He knew it was no use. But somehow his school bag was on the steps with the letters on top of it, and he was walking down towards the hens.

Chapter 21

SECRET'S END

The chookhouse was cool under its great load of passionfruit vine. The water system dripped . . . drop . . . drop . . . drop . . . into the water dish. There were chookprints in the mud all around it.

The water dish was always muddy, no matter how Harry redesigned it. He reckoned chooks were simply messy drinkers.

The hole was still there. Somehow Harry always half expected it to have disappeared now that Cissie had gone, but it still beamed as brightly as ever.

Harry made his way over to it slowly, as though

the slower he went the more time there might be for something — anything — to happen on the other side. He ducked under the perch, and pressed his eyes to the hole.

It was a grey day on the other side. The mist dusted the tops of the red gums, their trunks streaked pink and grey with damp. Harry knew that sort of day. The cold would soak through into your bones slowly, slowly, slowly, so it took hours to realise how were cold it really was, and then it would take hours to warm up again.

It was the sort of day when the chooks stalked across the flat and glared up at the house as though it was the humans who were responsible for the chill, cluckily demanding wheat and bread scraps and other bits of carbohydrate to keep them warm.

The creek was grey as well: mist grey, rock grey. There were no flowers on the waterlilies, no red gum blossom for bees to buzz in.

Something moved on the far bank. The wallaby, thought Harry. The one they'd seen before. Its face was damp, its paws were wet, as it bent its head to eat.

There was the rock where Cissie had sat the first day. There was Cissie's tree, with its gnarls that still looked like a face.

But not Cissie. He'd never see Cissie again.

Harry climbed the steps wearily. Days always seemed longer when it was hot.

'Harry? How was school? Did you remember the mail? Oh, good on you,' as Harry passed it over.

'What's for afternoon tea?' he asked.

'Bread and whatever,' said Mum absently, her eyes on the mail. 'The bananas need eating . . . bill from the garage, bank statement . . .'

Harry grabbed the cold water from the fridge and poured himself a drink. Mum had stuck some lemon peel in it to give it a tang. He drank the first glass quickly, then poured himself another.

'Did you see the postcard from Aunt Fran?' asked Mum. 'Pretty isn't it, all that sea . . . It must have taken nearly a fortnight to get here. She'd been home for over a week . . .

'Oh look, here's a photo from Stan and Maura's wedding, all the guests together outside the church. How lovely of them. You look so nice in your suit next to your father. I'll just stick it up here on the bureau till I can get it framed. Remind me next time we go into town.'

Harry gazed at the photo on the bureau. His hair looked stupid. He'd had it cut too short just before the wedding. He hoped that it looked better now. He sipped his drink slowly. Angie looked okay in that dress . . .

'Hey, Mum, what's this photo?' Harry peered at it more closely.

It was one of a dozen old ones Mum kept propped up at the back of the bureau, behind the gold cupid and the rock she'd found on her honeymoon and the china platypus he'd given her last Christmas and all the other ornaments. Somehow he'd never even thought to look at the photos before. They were too familiar to notice.

'Mmm? Oh that. That's great-uncle Merv and great-aunt Marg. *My* great-uncle Merv that is. He'd be your great-great-uncle. And that's Helen and Felicia — they're your grandmother's first cousins, my cousins once-removed. Helen's down in Melbourne and Fissy's up the Gold Coast. You know, you met her, Christmas before last when Uncle Steven . . .'

'What about this one? She looks like that dress is choking her.'

'That's a really old one. That'd be my great-grandmother. She was Welsh. Her maiden name was Edwards and . . .'

'How about this one?'

An old woman gazed at him, her eyes clear across the years. The photo was brown and white instead of black, and sort of faded. The frame was fancier than the others.

'The one on the end? That's even older. It's probably very precious. There were hardly any photographs in those days. She's on your dad's side of the family, not mine. His great-great . . . oh, I can't remember how many times grandmother. Yours, too, of course.

'She was the one who planted the oaks out the front, way back in the 1840's or fifties. She planted the Norfolk pines out by the shearing shed, too. What's her name again?'

Mum turned the photo over and looked at the back. 'Yes, here it is. Cecilia, I remember now. They called her Cissie, that was it. It's really Cissie's garden. That's what your gran told me when I first came here. Cissie was the one who planted the garden.'

Harry stared at the photo. It couldn't be. It was just coincidence. Probably there were lots of Cecilia's around then. And they might all have been nicknamed Cissie.

'Mum, what was her maiden name?'

'Goodness, I don't know. I don't suppose your dad would either. Wait a sec, I do know. It was Harrington. Cissie Harrington. I know because your great-great-grandfather owned a racehorse, oh, back at the turn of the century . . . the one that won all those prizes, and it was called Harrington's Pride, because it was descended from one of Cissie's. Your father's got a portrait of it in his office. Harrington, that was it.'

Harry was silent, looking at the picture.

It wasn't the girl in the hole, of course. This was an old woman, with hair that looked white in the brown and white photo. She looked happy, sitting there on a chair in the garden.

It must be her garden, thought Harry. Cissie

would want to be photographed in the garden she had planted.

'What happened to her?' he asked softly.

'I'm not sure. She had five kids, I think. Or was it seven? You'd have to ask your father, I'm just remembering what your great-gran told me. She was a great one for family history. They had big families in those days. And all of them lived, I think, which didn't happen often back then.'

'And Cissie married my great-something-grandad?'

'Of course,' said Mum. 'Otherwise you wouldn't be here.'

Of course.

Of course! It all made sense. Daniel — that kid — he must have been Daniel *Brookes*. My name, thought Harry . . . Dad's name . . . Grandad's name. Grandad was even called Dan. And their farm was Gran and Grandad's farm on the river, a long way away in those days, but only ten minutes by car today . . .

'It was a really romantic story,' said Mum. 'Your gran told it to me the first afternoon I came out here. I was still in High School and your dad had just got his driver's licence and this funny old Holden he'd bought with the money he got hay carting. I called it the Flying Wombat because it was brown, and your dad used to . . .'

'But what about Cissie, Mum!' insisted Harry.

'Cissie? Oh yes . . . Your gran was showing me round the garden, and she told me this story. This Cissie was an orphan, your gran said. Her father had been an officer at the garrison — you know, the old restaurant down by the river. We haven't been there for ages have we? Not since your gran's sixtieth birthday party. Then her father died, and her mother. There was talk of putting her in an orphanage down in Sydney, or even shipping her back to England to relatives there. But then she stayed here instead. They all paid for her to stay here.'

'Who?' asked Harry.

'The soldiers who were here. All of them together. The regiment. There was a fund or something, for the widows and orphans. What did your great-gran say about her? Some phrase she used . . . That's it. She was the daughter of the regiment.

'She stayed with a family down in Sydney for a while, so she could get an education. The soldiers all sent money every six months for her keep. Oh, and my pearl brooch — you know, the one I wear at Christmas? That was hers, too. See, she's wearing it in the photo. It's all coming back to me now.

'She was an orphan, and the garrison was being withdrawn. It was only here in the first place because they were worried that the French might invade, but of course they didn't. Anyway, after they left and went back to England Cissie was put to board down in Sydney, but she spent her holidays up here with your great-something-grandad's parents. And your great-something-grandad, of course.

'Well, they fell in love and she married him when she turned eighteen, and they selected this place and built this house — or the main part of it, anyway, your great-grandad added the back bit — and Cissie planted her garden. All the big trees are hers. Oh, and the hedge along the drive, of course.

'The blokes in the regiment sent the brooch out to her when she got married. Every time the eldest son marries it's given to his wife. Your gran gave it to me that first Christmas after your father and I were married — you were born just three months later, just two weeks before your dad's birthday. You'll give Cissie's brooch to your wife some day I suppose,' said Mum smiling.

'So she's been here all the time,' said Harry slowly. 'She left, but she came back. She's been here all along, there on the bureau.'

But of course she'd been here in other ways as well . . .

Mum blinked.

'What do you mean?' she asked.

'Nothing. Nothing at all,' said Harry. 'Are there any more photos of her, Mum?'

'I'm not sure,' said Mum. 'People didn't have their photo taken very often in those days. A photographer probably only came to this district once every few years. Your gran would know. Ask her at lunch next Sunday if you're curious. It's a nice story, isn't it? The daughter of the regiment.'

'Yeah,' said Harry. 'It's a nice story, Mum.'

Harry waited till Mum had gone down to the vegetable garden to pick silver beet for dinner. Then he went to the phone.

Angie would understand. Angie understood a lot of things.

'Hello? It's Harry speaking. Can I speak to Angie?' he asked. 'Angie. It's me. It's Harry. She's all right, Angie. She's all right.'

It was cool on the verandah after dinner. Harry sat on the banana lounge and watched the leaf shadows shake over the lawn. The tin on the chookhouse roof gleamed in the last of the light. The hole would be almost faded now, waiting for tomorrow's light, the light that shone from more than a hundred years away.

What would he see through the hole tomorrow. Next year, ten years time? And what might his children see?

His great-whatsit-grandfather maybe, and Cissie, building their house? Or even dad, or grandad. Or himself and Angie, swimming in the creek, when they too had become the past.

He would leave, like Cissie had. And, like Cissie, he'd come back. The oak leaves shuddered as the breeze grew with the dark. The oaks would have been small in Cissie's time. Cissie's oaks . . .

She would have sat here last century and watched the trees she'd planted. The hills would have looked the same, the dark sky and the moon . . .

She was happy here, thought Harry. It had been part of her, like it was part of him. No matter where he went, or what he did, this land would always in some way still be his.

'Goodnight Cissie,' he said.